Carol Marinelli

BOUGHT BY THE
BILLIONAIRE PRINCE

TORONTO • NEW YORK • LONDON
AMSTERDAM • PARIS • SYDNEY • HAMBURG
STOCKHOLM • ATHENS • TOKYO • MILAN • MADRID
PRAGUE • WARSAW • BUDAPEST • AUCKLAND

For Sam, Alex and Lucinda
with all my love xxx

ISBN-13: 978-0-373-12659-0
ISBN-10:   0-373-12659-X

BOUGHT BY THE BILLIONAIRE PRINCE

First North American Publication 2007.

Copyright © 2007 by Harlequin Books S.A.

Special thanks and acknowledgment are given to Carol Marinelli for her contribution to THE ROYAL HOUSE OF NIROLI series.

The Rules

Rule 1: The ruler must be a moral leader. Any act that brings the Royal House into disrepute will rule a contender out of the succession to the throne.

Rule 2: No member of the Royal House may be joined in marriage without consent of the ruler. Any such union results in exclusion and deprivation of honors and privileges.

Rule 3: No marriage is permitted if the interests of Niroli become compromised through the union.

Rule 4: It is not permitted for the ruler of Niroli to marry a person who has previously been divorced.

Rule 5: Marriage between members of the Royal House who are blood relations is forbidden.

Rule 6: The ruler directs the education of all members of the Royal House, even when the general care of the children belongs to their parents.

Rule 7: Without the approval or consent of the ruler, no member of the Royal House can make debts over the possibility of payment.

Rule 8: No member of the Royal House can accept an inheritance or any donation without the consent and approval of the ruler.

Rule 9: The ruler of Niroli must dedicate their life to the Kingdom. Therefore they are not permitted to have a profession.

Rule 10: Members of the Royal House must reside in Niroli or in a country approved by the ruler. However, the ruler *must* reside in Niroli.

THE ROYAL HOUSE OF NIROLI

Always passionate, always proud.

Each month, Harlequin Presents is delighted
to bring you an exciting installment from
THE ROYAL HOUSE OF NIROLI, in which you can
follow the epic search for the true Nirolian king.
Eight heirs, eight romances, eight fantastic stories!

The Future King's Pregnant Mistress
by Penny Jordan

Surgeon Prince, Ordinary Wife
by Melanie Milburne

Bought by the Billionaire Prince
by Carol Marinelli

Coming next month

The Tycoon's Princess Bride
by Natasha Oakley
Isabella has always known that she cannot marry
only for love: if she is to be crowned queen, she must
be betrothed to a man of the King's choice!

Expecting His Royal Baby
by Susan Stephens

The Prince's Forbidden Virgin
by Robyn Donald

Bride by Royal Appointment
by Raye Morgan

A Royal Bride at the Sheikh's Command
by Penny Jordan

CHAPTER ONE

'Is HE good-looking?'

Meg felt her teeth literally grind together as her travel companion, Jasmine, repeated the question for the hundredth time. Here they were docking in Niroli, which was undoubtedly the most beautiful island Meg had seen on her travels to date, and all Jasmine wanted to talk about was potential men.

Coming from Australia, where everything was comparatively new, Meg was in awe of the past that drenched each place she had visited on her travels through Europe, reeling at the ancient architecture and glorious tales of times gone by and, for Meg, Niroli had it all! To the South of Sicily, the island of Niroli, according to the travel guide Meg had devoured on the boat trip, was steeped in history, its colourful past filled with rivalries and wars dating back centuries and still playing out today. They'd just passed the tiny island of Mont Avellana, which, as recently as two decades ago, had been ruled by Niroli, and now they were coming into Niroli's main port. Meg stared in wonder as they approached—sandy beaches rapidly giving way to a lush hillside, which was like a fabulous tapestry, with thick forests, and edged by vineyards that laced neatly around the sprawling town. But a grand castle set on a rocky promontory was for Meg the main focal point, standing tall and proud, looking out towards the ocean, as if somehow guarding it all.

'That's the palace,' Meg pointed out to Jasmine excitedly, checking with the map to get her bearings, 'and over to the right there's a Roman amphitheatre….'

'There's a casino,' Jasmine said, peering over Meg's shoulder, 'oh, and a luxury spa!'

'We can't afford luxury.' Meg smiled. 'We're backpacking!'

'Then we'll just have to find someone who can!' Jasmine countered, her mind flicking back to the inevitable. 'So what sort of doctor is he?'

'Who?' Meg asked, then let out a pained sigh as Jasmine's momentary interest in her surrounds rapidly waned. 'Alex is a surgeon,' Meg admitted, then wished she hadn't, noting Jasmine's eyes literally light up at the prospect of dating a rich surgeon—well, she could dream on. Alex was the least money-minded of persons and would see through Jasmine in a flash.

If only she had, Meg inwardly sighed. At first when Jasmine had befriended her, Meg had been only too glad of the company, only lately the very qualities that Meg had admired had started to repel. Jasmine's impetuous nature, her carefree attitude and her obsession with men were starting to irritate, and Meg was actually looking forward to cooling off the friendship a touch—ready now to complete her journey alone.

Backpacking through Europe had seemed the most unlikely of adventures for Meg to embark on. Routine was the key in Meg's life—routine was what saw her through. Routine was the only way she could control her life and the emotions that had overwhelmed her as she'd struggled to come to terms with her difficult childhood.

But now here she was, twenty-five years of age and ready to start living; ready to let go of a difficult past and truly embrace a world that had at times been so very cruel. Backpacking through Europe was the final self-imposed step in her recovery. Casual work, casual clothes and casual meals had at first been a huge enigma for Meg, but gradually she was starting to relax—that knot of tension that had been present for as long as she could remember was slowly unravelling and, as she stepped off the boat and took a deep cleansing breath, closed her blue eyes and turned her face up to the warm sun Meg knew there and then that she had been so right to embark on this journey—could hardly wait to tell her brother just how far she'd come.

'Where is he?' Jasmine's hopeful face scanned the crowd for a first glimpse of a suitable good-looking surgeon. 'Does he look like you?'

'Not in the least.' Meg laughed but didn't elaborate. Alex Hunter was as dark as Meg Donovan was blond, his eyes black where Meg's were blue. They looked nothing alike and with good reason—both were adopted, Alex when he was a toddler, Meg when she was twelve years old. But despite their differences, despite not sharing one shred of DNA, they were as close as any blood brother and sister.

'Does he know what boat you're coming on?'

'I told him ages ago.' Meg frowned. 'Well, I emailed him with the details.'

'And he got it?' Jasmine checked.

'Yes, I'm sure he got it,' Meg answered, but a trickle of unease slid down her spine. 'He *should* be here.'

'Well, it doesn't look like he is,' Jasmine pointed out as the crowd started to disperse. 'Maybe he's stuck at the hospital.'

'Maybe,' Meg answered, but she wasn't convinced. It

was *most* unlike Alex to just not turn up; if he couldn't make it himself then he'd have sent someone. 'Though I haven't checked my emails for ages. Maybe he's been trying to get hold of me.'

'So what do we do now?' Jasmine asked, her eyes scanning the notice boards. 'They said at the youth hostel there were usually loads of signs advertising for seasonal workers, but there doesn't seem to be any—not that I fancy fruit-picking!'

'It sounds fun. And you *do* need the work,' Meg pointed out. Jasmine wasn't just down to her last Euro, she was dipping into Meg's carefully planned budget and, frankly, Meg was tired of hearing Jasmine say she'd pay her back as soon as she got some work.

'Well, I think fruit-picking sounds awful.' Jasmine pouted, but soon cheered up, cheekily ripping down a notice and then pocketing it. 'This is more me. They're looking for casual staff at the casino and there's discounted accommodation—ooh, look, there's even a courtesy bus.'

'I think that's for the clientele,' Meg said as some holiday-makers who certainly weren't backpackers were escorted into the luxury vehicle.

'So?' Jasmine shrugged and pulled on her backpack as she called to the bus driver to wait for her—Meg couldn't help but smile; Jasmine was like a cat who always landed on her feet. 'Come on, Meg.'

'I don't think so.' Meg shook her head. 'A casino is the *last* place I want to be. All that noise and bustle…'

'All those rich men!' Jasmine giggled and even Meg managed a laugh. 'Come on, Meg, hold off on your search for inner peace for a few days and come and have some fun at the casino. We can share a room.'

'It's really not me.' Raking a hand through her blond hair, Meg felt the salt and grease and almost relented—given Alex wasn't here, that long soak in a bath she'd been looking forward to wasn't going to eventuate and accommodation at the casino, even if it was budget accommodation, was surely going to be better than some of the hostels she'd stayed in. 'I think I'll head over to the hospital.' Meg checked out her map. 'It isn't very far. Maybe he *is* just caught up at work. You'd better go or you're going to miss that courtesy bus.'

'Well, if it doesn't work out with your brother, you know where I am.'

'Thanks.' Meg grinned, watching as her friend climbed on the bus and waved her off, wishing, *wishing* she could, even for a little while, be as happy and as carefree as Jasmine—could relax just a little bit, could have just a fraction of her confidence. The universe itself seemed to provide Jasmine with her assured nature.

Meg watched until the tiny bus disappeared from view, filled with something she couldn't define—a hunger, a need almost for familiarity, to be able to let down her guard a touch, to be with someone who knew how hard this was for her, someone who knew that this so-called trip of a lifetime, this carefree existence, was in fact an agonising journey for her.

Where the hell was Alex?

The last e-mail he'd sent, he'd confirmed her date and time of arrival, had told her he couldn't wait to catch up, had huge news to share. Surely if his plans had changed he'd have contacted her?

But how?

Meg closed her eyes against a temporary moment of panic. She hadn't been near a computer for the last couple of weeks—happy the next leg of her tour had been arranged, she'd decided to cut loose for a while—and look where it had got her!

The taxi rank had long since closed, so, consulting her map, Meg set out on foot towards the Free Hospital where Alex had told her he was working. The midday sun combined with her heavy backpack made the relatively short distance seem to take for ever. How she'd have loved to have lingered and wandered through the pretty shops, but a backpack and a pressing lack of accommodation for the night didn't allow for such luxuries, so instead Meg stopped at one of the pavement cafés and ordered a quick coffee. Watching intrigued as the town seemingly prepared for something—shopkeepers were draping their stores with huge vines, hilarity ensuing as a few vocal locals strung banners and lights across the street, calling to each other in their colourful language as children watched on gleefully.

'Is there going to be a party?' Meg asked one of waiters whose English was better than most.

'A bigger party than you have ever seen!' Filling her cup he elaborated, 'The Niroli Feast starts tomorrow—we party for the next few days and celebrate the treasures the rich soil gives us.'

'Here?' Meg checked, gesturing to the street they were in, but the waiter just laughed.

'The whole island celebrates—you *must* stay for it,' he insisted as only the Italians could. 'I ask you—why would anyone not want to stay a while in this wonderful place?'

Why indeed?

Boosted from her shot of coffee, Meg made her way more briskly to the hospital, hoping against hope that Alex would be there and trying to fathom what she'd do if he wasn't.

* * *

'Dr Alex Hunter!' Meg tried to keep her voice even, trying not to show her frustration as she said her brother's name for perhaps the tenth time. On perhaps the eleventh, the receptionist nodded her immaculately groomed head.

'*Sì*, Alessandro Fierezza!' Eagerly, again she nodded, tapping details into her computer. 'He no here, I have no contact for him. Try *palazzo!*'

Help!

Meg grabbed her long hair into a tight fist and let out an exasperated breath as the receptionist called on a colleague, who spoke even less English, listening to their vibrant discussion peppered with the names Alex and Alessandro and wondering what on earth she should do.

'Your brother marry.'

'But my brother is not married, he's not even engaged!' Meg gave a helpless laugh, then shook her head as in broken English the two women attempted to explain the impossible.

'*Matrimonio,*' the receptionist said firmly, nodding as Meg frowned. 'Your brother, Alessandro—'

'Alex,' Meg corrected, then slumped in defeat as the receptionist forced her to admit the truth—even if they had got the names mixed up, the simple fact was if Alex was in Niroli then he'd have met her at the port; her careful plans for the next couple of weeks flying out of the window courtesy of three little words—

'Your brother gone.'

CHAPTER TWO

JASMINE HAD BEEN RIGHT—there *was* work at the casino.

Lots of it!

Working her way through mountain after mountain of white china plates, Meg tried to block out the noise of a busy kitchen—the chefs screaming at each other like proud cats fighting over territory, waiters collecting elaborate dishes, swooshing out of the swing doors only to return moments later, laden with half-eaten dishes to add to the pile Meg had been allocated. Not that Meg minded hard work, she'd been more than prepared for the back-breaking work of fruit-picking, but being shut up in a kitchen, her face red from the heat, her blond hair dark with sweat, was a million miles from what she'd envisaged from her time in Niroli.

Almost as soon as she'd found Jasmine and filled in an application form, Meg had been given a list of shifts. Six till ten o'clock each evening, paid in cash at the end of each of shift, which meant Meg had the whole day for exploring Niroli, and it paid well, *much* better than fruit-picking, which meant, Meg realised, if she was careful and perhaps worked a couple of extra shifts she could treat herself to a day at that luxury spa.

With renewed enthusiasm Meg tackled the mountain of

plates—the last hour of her shift made so much easier by fantasising about being smeared in the famous Niroli volcanic mud she'd read about and being thoroughly pampered and spoiled for a day!

'Faster now!' Antoinette, her colleague for the night who was rinsing and stacking the plates that Meg was washing, egged her on in her broken English, but kindly. 'We need empty sink for next staff. Or else they…' She didn't finish what she was saying—in fact a ream of sentences and orders around the kitchen remained forever incomplete, broken off midword for a reason Meg couldn't yet fathom—the swing doors opened and an immediate hush descended on the busy kitchen as a group of dark suits entered.

'Ah—sir!' The head chef jumped to nervous attention as he approached the foreboding-looking men that had entered, yet he addressed only the leader.

And even if he hadn't uttered a single word, even if she had no idea who he was, Meg knew that he was very much in charge. His jet hair was a head above the rest of them, but it wasn't just his height that set him apart—there was an authoritative air about him that would hush any room, an intimidating and overwhelming presence that had everyone in the kitchen, Meg included, on heightened alert.

'Who is he?' Meg whispered to Antoinette as slowly he toured the kitchen, talking with the staff as he did so. There was a slightly depraved look to him, a dangerous glint in those black eyes as he worked the room.

'That,' Antoinette said, in broken English, 'is the boss, Luca Fierezza. He owns the casino. A prince.'

For a simple woman like Antoinette, Meg reasoned, such an enigmatic personality *would* seem like a prince. Not for a second did it enter her head that *nothing* had been lost in translation.

He was over at the far end now, talking with some of the kitchen staff, and Meg quickly realised that this was far more than a cursory appearance by the owner, that he was actually listening to what they were saying, taking in every word and relaying them to one of his sidekicks who was faithfully writing down each word.

'He comes often,' Antoinette said. 'He make sure that everything work okay. See, now Mario tell him the trouble we are having with the shrimp—the yield was low this last two days….'

'Is that his concern?' When Antoinette frowned Meg attempted to make herself clearer. 'Isn't that a problem for the kitchen?'

'He makes it his concern,' Antoinette said, an almost proud note to her voice as she did, letting Meg know she had understood her the first time. 'This casino is the best place to play and to work—Luca makes sure of that. I work here under four different owners and he is the best.

'Come—' she nudged Meg '—work now. He is coming.'

Meg could feel him making his way over, feel the thick tension in the air as he worked the room, the raucous sound of the earlier kitchen replaced now by the quiet hum of ordered efficiency.

'Antoinette!' he greeted the elderly lady by her first name. *'Come stai?'* How are you?

'Molto bene, grazie.' Very well, thank you. Antoinette carried on working as she spoke, kept her head down as she addressed her boss, but, Meg noted, even if his greeting had been personable and friendly, Antoinette was keeping her respectful distance, a clear pecking order on display.

Meg glanced over as he walked past, gave him a brief polite nod as he did the same, and then picked up a plate, swishing the cloth over it, waiting for him to move on—a casual kitchen hand undoubtedly didn't merit Antoinette's more familiar greeting—only he didn't move on! Meg could feel him standing over her shoulder; feel the burn of his eyes on the back of her neck as he questioned Antoinette.

Antoinette introduced Meg and he asked something in Italian, his rich, fluid voice prompting Meg to briefly turn around.

'She's a good worker,' Antoinette responded to his question as Luca ran a dismissive eye over her, and, turning her back on him, Meg plunged her hands back into the soapy water, her skin red—not from heat or exertion, instead embarrassment, humiliation prickling every nerve as they openly discussed her without inclusion.

She was beautiful.

Luca had noticed her the second he'd walked into the kitchen, her blond head amidst the many dark ones immediately drawing his attention, her tall, willowy body forcing his gaze.

She didn't belong in the kitchen—that tall, delicate frame would wear the finest of gowns with ease; those long, delicate fingers should be wrapped around the silverware on the other side of the door; those full lips should be tasting the delicacies produced here, not clearing the aftermath. Yet she clearly thought otherwise. There was nothing martyred in her stance as she worked on, unlike some of the foreigners who came to the island—he had met one just moments before. Bold as brass, she had deemed herself too good for the manual work behind the scenes.

Only *this* lady *was* too good for this.

Too good for here, only she didn't know it yet—and now she was turning her back on him.

Luca felt the discomfort of his staff around him, registered the appalled look on Antoinette's face as this *Meg* broke with protocol as she turned her slender back to him and proceeded to work on, but instead of feeling enraged, instead of demanding that she face him when he spoke, unusually he smiled and took a step closer to her. For the first time he inhaled the scent of her and it was like pulling the stopper on a fragrance bottle, a heady rush of femininity filling his nostrils, his first instinct to touch her shoulder, to turn her around to face him, but he resisted. Instead he clenched his fingers into his palms—there would be time for that later.

There would be a later.

Luca knew that with the certainty of a man who always got his own way. A combination of wealth, power and devilish good looks were a heady cocktail no woman had ever refused—at least not for long. The pleasure of pursuit was a skill Luca never needed for more than the short-term. But chatting up a lowly kitchen hand was far from Luca's style, so quickly he came up with what *he* deemed a suitable solution, addressing her for the first time in English.

'We need blondes out on the casino floor. You come and see me tomorrow and we can discuss something—'

'No, thank you,' Meg interrupted, still keeping her back to him, still not looking at him, but at least she was moving now—quickly washing the dishes, anger fuelling her, appalled at the gall of him.

'I am offering you a promotion.'

'And I'm declining,' Meg answered through gritted teeth,

her hand reaching for the hose to rinse the plates and sorely tempted to turn it on him, but Luca wasn't about to be dismissed, his voice authoritative, almost daring her to defy him.

'You will turn around and face me when I speak with you.'

Oh, she'd face him, all right, Meg decided, swinging her *blond* head around, more than ready to give him a piece of her mind, more than ready to tell him just what he could do with his blatant chauvinism, but again she hadn't counted on the effect of Luca up close and personal.

He was savagely good-looking.

Savage, because the effect of him close up was utterly brutal—like staring into the sun. His beauty, his presence was so dazzling, so blinding that, though the sensible thing to do was surely tear her eyes away, to shield herself from his effect, Meg found it impossible. Instead, she took in the impeccable attire, the raven hair without even a fleck of silver, and his exquisitely chiselled face that hadn't met with a razor for the last couple of days, the dark stubble of regrowth giving him a bandit-like appearance.

Danger!

Her mind was screaming it, playing out the message in stereo in her head, yet for once her body wasn't listening. Instead it was flaming into a wicked response caused by a mere look from him and now burning with awareness as his eyes leisurely worked her, leaving Meg to beg the perilous question as to how she would respond if he so much as touched her.

'I'd prefer to work in the kitchen…' Her voice was a croak, her protest pathetically weak compared to the one she had intended, but Luca wasn't listening anyway.

'You work where I tell you to. Nine o'clock tomorrow.' His thickly accented voice clipped his order and Meg stiffened. 'You come and see me then, tell the security staff who you are when you arrive and they will show you where to go—oh, and wear something nice.'

'Lucky you.' Antoinette beamed as Luca stalked out of the kitchen followed by his entourage, but normal services were definitely not resumed, every member of the kitchen crew staring at her, awaiting her reaction as Antoinette excitedly chatted on. 'Tomorrow you will be working on the casino floor—'

'I don't want to,' Meg broke in. 'I've already told him that!' But Antoinette firmly shook her head, her voice more insistent now.

'You will do as Luca says. You *have* to go and see him—he has ordered you.'

'He can order away,' Meg said grimly, peeling off her drenched apron as Antoinette did the same, the long, exhausting shift over, and even as they took their work cards to the management and were paid for their time, somehow Meg knew that tonight had been her first and final foray as a kitchen hand at the Niroli casino, that when she didn't turn up tomorrow for *promotion*, her services would no longer be required.

But it wasn't a lack of work that was troubling Meg.

It was the effect *that* look had had on her—the fact that, despite her brave words, despite his appalling rudeness, she was actually *thinking* of going to see him again tomorrow.

Meg practically ran back to her hotel room, ran as if the devil himself were chasing her, but she couldn't outrun her feelings, shocking emotions beating her to her door.

With one look, one brief exchange, it was as if he'd somehow reached inside and flicked a switch, aroused feelings that were so deeply buried Meg was barely aware of their existence—till now. It was as if he'd undressed her right there in the kitchen with his black, knowing eyes, as if in the two seconds he'd graced her with, somehow he had peeled away every layer of clothing, leaving her vulnerable and exposed. And if ever it were possible to make love to someone and never even touch them, then that was surely what had just happened.

Tomorrow morning she'd pack her things and head to Mont Avellana, look for work in the vineyards or orange groves. She was tired of Jasmine anyway; it wasn't running away, Meg countered her own question as her shaking hand put the key in the lock.

It was about staying in control.

CHAPTER THREE

'COME ON, Meg—loosen up and live a little!'

Since Meg had arrived back from her shift Jasmine had been attempting to persuade her to dress up and venture out to explore the night life on their doorstep, but it was positively the *last* thing Meg felt like doing. They'd been travelling since the early morning, she'd worked in the hot kitchen and that was all on top of the disappointment of missing Alex. Stepping out of the shower and falling into bed were the only things on her mind; except it was their last night together and *loosen up and live a little* had been the exact reasons for this trip. Though she might be travelling lightly, Meg's emotional baggage was weighty and few would ever know the supreme effort it took for Meg to give a casual shrug of her shoulders and finally nod in agreement. 'Just for a couple of hours,' Meg warned, peeling open her backpack and peering inside.

'Well, hurry up and don't take for ever deciding what to wear!'

Which was a joke only backpackers could understand! In an attempt to travel lightly, Meg had packed only one outfit suitable for a glamorous night out—which on the positive side removed the usual angst of what to wear, whilst on the down side…

What had she been thinking when she'd packed it?

The short black tube skirt had seemed a good choice when packing as it took up a mere square inch of her backpack, and the crushed silk azure top took up even less space; only they showed off way more of her body than Meg really felt comfortable with—the confident, assured woman she had envisaged wearing these was probably a few weeks further into her getting her life together.

Stepping back, Meg **stared at** her reflection, took in the slender, tanned body, he**r hair** scooped up and twisted into a casual but elegant style. Her face that had been void of make-up for her entire trip seemed unfamiliar now—her blue eyes sparkling vividly with the help of shimmering eye shadow and a slick of black mascara, high cheekbones accentuated with a hint of rouge and her lips plump and full with the help of some lipstick. But despite the vision that stared back at her, despite the transformation that had taken place in the small, cramped bathroom, still Meg eyed herself critically, fighting the urge to rip off the clothes, to rub off the make-up, to dive into her bed and pull the sheet over her head. She almost *hated* the woman who stared back at her, the confident, feminine, sultry image that belied the terrified child inside, her exposed flesh, the curves on her body, the jutting, high breasts, provoking terror within her. She knew that tonight she'd turn heads, that men would look at her, men like Luca....

Her throat felt tight as she swallowed hard, forced herself to relive that brief encounter. She could feel his eyes burning her skin all over again, the shock of sexual awareness fizzing through her body no matter how she'd tried to douse it. Since she'd first glimpsed him, since first he'd stepped closer into her personal space, Meg had felt unsettled, as if he'd

taken some imaginary spoon and skillfully stirred her somewhere deep inside.

He was beautiful—even that blatantly obvious acknowledgement was a monumental feat for Meg, a step forward
even. Too many times in the past she'd buried her feelings,
refused to examine them, but standing there staring at her reflection, her knuckles white as she gripped the sink, Meg
forced herself to stay with her feelings for a moment—to
explore them. Those dark, liquid silk eyes had caressed her,
the deep drawl of his voice had moved her, and Meg acknowledged how much she *had* wanted to take him up on
his offer, and find out what exactly he had in store for her...to
see him again!

'No!'

She said the word out loud, pulled the window shut on
the thoughts that were flittering in. He wanted her for how
she looked—could look; he'd made that blatantly clear. Men
like Luca were used to getting what they wanted, most
women couldn't resist their charms.

Only she wasn't like most women.

'You look fantastic!' Jasmine thrust a glass of cheap wine
into her hand as Meg stepped out from the bathroom. 'I
adore your top. Where did you get it?'

'At a craft market in Queensland.' Meg attempted girl-
talk, tried and wished to be as happy and carefree as Jasmine
as they discussed her top; mind you, it was divine. The
deepest azure, it scooped into a halter neck and from the front
it looked elegant and simple, but it was rather more daring
from behind, its low cut making the wearing of a bra impossible and instead revealing the vast expanse of her golden
sun-kissed back and almost the entire column of her vertebra.

The crushed silk fabric was caught at the bottom and ruched together in a glittering butterfly encrusted with glass beads and semiprecious stones. The moment Meg had set eyes on it she'd wanted it—one of the few impulse buys in her life.

'Well, you look stunning,' Jasmine affirmed with a slight hiccough as she forced down her wine. 'Why on earth do you hide yourself away all the time?'

'I don't,' Meg clipped, refusing to accept the compliment and certainly not answering the question. Instead, she took a sip of the drink and screwed up her face, wondering how Jasmine managed to drink it as if it were flavoured water. Her heart rate seemed to be topping a hundred and Meg knew that if they didn't leave now, then she'd surely change her mind. 'Come on, Jasmine—let's hit the town!'

The casino was everything Meg had expected it would be and more. The white marble of the floors and walls in the vast foyer, where Jasmine and Meg stood getting their bearings, was no doubt a cool respite from the activity in the gaming rooms.

Despite the lateness of hour, it hummed with activity, elevators pinging regularly as winners and losers spilled out, heading to the bars and restaurants eager to spend their winnings or drown their sorrows, the sound of machines an ever-present backdrop. Jasmine and Meg wandered a while, peering into the designer shops, noses pressed against the windows like children at a toy shop.

'He's going to buy it for her!' Jasmine breathed, watching as a rather ancient gentlemen leant heavily on his walking frame with one hand as his other retrieved a wallet, peeling off one of many credit cards and handing it to a pouting redhead who was young enough to be his granddaughter. 'He's actually going to buy that diamond ring for her! Lucky, lucky thing!'

'Lucky?' Meg screwed up her nose in distaste, not sure who to feel sorry for—the woman who would later *pay* an extremely high price for her gift or the man who was being fleeced.

'Let's go in.' Jasmine nudged Meg, pressing the intercom and waving at the assistant who gave a snooty frown as she looked over.

'I somehow don't think we're the kind of clientele they're looking for,' Meg said, turning to go, but just as she did, surprisingly the assistant came over, gesturing to a security guard who opened the heavy glass door. Like a puppy chasing a ball, Jasmine leapt inside as Meg rather more hesitantly entered.

'Is there anything in particular you are looking for?' The assistant spoke fluent English and directed all of her questions at Meg. Embarrassed, Meg shook her head.

'We're just browsing—if that's okay?'

'Of course!'

But browsing in an exclusive jewellery shop in the Niroli casino was nothing like the high-street stores Meg usually frequented. In fact, it was like nowhere Meg had ever been in her life. Once inside, the rather snooty demeanour of the receptionist faded—slivers of bitter chocolate were offered and refused, but a glass of champagne thrust into her hand while *looking* was apparently non-negotiable—but Meg couldn't relax and enjoy. Excruciatingly aware of the security cameras whirring and homing in, and more than aware she couldn't afford as much as a keyring, all Meg wanted was out.

But Jasmine had other ideas. 'Oh, would you look at these? Have you ever seen anything as beautiful?'

Never.

Peering into the glass display cabinet, even Meg, who was itching to escape, was momentarily transfixed; on simple black velvet hung a pendant and earrings and, even to a novice like Meg, their worth was clearly more than the entire shop put together.

'They are very beautiful, yes?'

'Stunning!' Meg watched as her breath fogged up the glass, eyes widening as the assistant pulled out a key from her belt and opened the display cabinet.

'Clearly you appreciate the finer things—these are pieces from some of the Niroli royal family's collection. You can hold them for a moment—but that is all.'

'We can actually hold them?' Meg blinked.

'The king tries to make things more...' The assistant snapped her fingers as she attempted to locate the word she was looking for, and then settled for a longer version. 'He tries to let his people closer to the family—these are not the best pieces, of course.'

And this wasn't your average jeweller's, Meg thought. They were locked in, cameras were everywhere, but even so holding such treasures even for a short while was a rare treat.

'How much are they worth?' Jasmine asked as the assistant placed the jewels in Meg's hands, the cool of the perfect stones heavy in her heated palms, and Meg knew the answer before the assistant even spoke.

'They are not for sale. We are honoured to have them for a short while.'

'They must be insured for a figure,' Jasmine rudely pushed as Meg handed the treasures back.

'Their street value is not relevant,' the assistant answered tartly. 'These jewels stay within the royal family.'

* * *

'Snooty madam!' Jasmine declared once they were outside. 'I wonder what they are worth…'

'What does it matter?' Meg asked. 'I can't believe we actually got to hold them—I wish I'd brought my camera.'

'You probably wouldn't have been allowed to use it,' Jasmine pointed out. 'Right, enough of window-shopping. I'm tired of looking at things I'll never be able to afford!'

'Let's go and buy a drink,' Meg suggested.

'Let's not!' Jasmine laughed, steering a bemused Meg out of the shopping mall and through a gaming room towards a bar. Supremely self-conscious, Meg took a seat on a bar stool, pulling her skirt down over her thighs, then fiddling with her earrings, aware that they had been noticed. More than a few heads had turned as they'd walked into the room but, instead of boosting Meg's confidence, it merely heightened her already nervous state, especially when Jasmine assuredly summoned the bartender and loudly ordered two glasses of their most expensive champagne.

'We're on a budget,' Meg whimpered, aware that the slender glass the waiter was pouring the pale golden liquid into was undoubtedly worth her entire night's spending money.

'Relax, will you?' Jasmine giggled, pulling a sequinned purse out of her evening bag, but before she'd even opened the zipper, before the drinks had even been put down on the placemats, the bartender halted her.

'It has already been taken care of.' He gestured to a nearby table, where four middle-aged businessmen sat, staring openly at them with knowing smiles.

'Salute!'

'Cheers!' Jasmine held her glass up in acknowledgement

to the nearby table, then winked at an appalled Meg. 'Come on, drink up. There'll be plenty more where that came from.'

'At what price, though?' Meg bit the words out—she could feel the colour mounting on her cheeks, torn between wanting to send the drinks back and not wanting to make a scene. 'Jasmine, they're going to want something….'

'Oh, for heaven's sake, Meg! Will you loosen up? For God's sake, they bought us a drink. Can't you just say thank you? It's just a bit of fun.'

Only it wasn't.

As Meg had predicted, as soon as the glasses met their lips the men made their way over, sleazy chat-up lines were followed by sleazy chat-up lines, a bottle of champagne soon appeared, and all she wanted was to get the hell out, knowing the money that was being spent on them had nothing to do with their engaging conversation, nothing to do with a man wanting to get to know a woman. It had been a mistake to come—a horrible, horrible mistake.

'They want us to play the tables!' Jasmine said gleefully as Meg bit back a smart retort. 'Come on!'

She was tired of pointing things out to Jasmine—tired of acting like a boring big sister when Jasmine clearly didn't want to hear what she had to say.

'I'm going to bed.'

'Bed!' Jasmine gave her a wide-eyed look. 'It isn't even midnight. Come on, Meg. It will be fun.'

'It's not my kind of fun,' Meg answered. 'Look, Jasmine, I'm tired and I don't particularly like the company we're keeping. If you want to stay on, then that's up to you. Just be careful.'

'Five minutes,' Jasmine pleaded. 'Then slip away— pretend you're going to the loo or something.'

They were already at the gaming area, Jasmine's eyes glittering from the champagne and attention as Meg attempted her excuses. There was nothing subtle now about the men's advances—one of them offered her a chip to play the roulette table, which Meg refused, a prickle of fear running down her spine as Jasmine accepted. Things were really starting to get out of control.

'Thirty, red.' Jasmine kissed her chip and placed it on the table as Meg watched on. She'd never played roulette. Oh, she'd seen it on films, but she had no idea of the rules and absolutely no desire to find out, but her escort was insistent, pushing the chip into her hand.

'No!' Meg almost shouted the word and flung the beastly chip at him. She wanted nothing from him, nothing at all. And, boring or not, she was going to get Jasmine out of here and tell her she was flirting with danger. Once this beastly game was over, even if she had to frog-march her to the toilet, *that* was what she was going to do!

'Your bet, please.'

As the businessman who had latched onto Meg pushed the chip back into her hand, Meg again shook her head, but table etiquette demanded she now play, and if Meg didn't want to make a scene then she had no option but to place her bet. 'Black seventeen,' she said, plucking a number from midair and pulling out her purse, refusing to baulk when the croupier informed her of the minimum bet and handing over her entire night's wages plus a touch more.

Meg barely watched as the wheel spun. Her eyes were seemingly on it, but her mind was elsewhere. Sensing the leering stares of her companions, feeling a hand lingering too long as it brushed her back, she wished this moment over, willed the ball to stop anywhere, for this awful night to end.

Tomorrow she was leaving…. The wheel was slowing down as her jumbled thoughts assimilated into some sort of order, her mind calming as she worked out a rudimentary plan: her job in the kitchen was over, when she didn't show up in Luca's office tomorrow she'd be out on her ear anyway, and tonight Jasmine had delivered the last straw. She was tired of Jasmine, tired of Niroli come to that—she'd had nothing but trouble and disappointment since she'd arrived. First thing tomorrow she'd head to back to the port, catch a boat to Mont Avellana perhaps. She'd heard there was seasonal work there…. Only the ball was moving now, rattling around the stilling wheel and even though the tension at the table was building, now she had a plan, for Meg it was abating….

Until the ball landed in its slot and all hell broke loose.

Black, seventeen!

CHAPTER FOUR

'TABLE FOUR; move in closer!'

Luca's order was swiftly obeyed, the security camera zooming in on the minor commotion in the general public gaming room, the winning figure being relayed to Dario, his Chief of Security, through an earpiece and passed on to Luca, who didn't bat an eyelid. It was small pickings compared to the figures he dealt with on a daily and nightly basis and, more to the point, in a few hours the winnings would most probably be fed back into the casino. No, it wasn't the money that intrigued Luca, it was the reaction of the women that held his attention now. One was jumping up and down, accepting champagne and kisses in all directions, and for a moment Luca thought the information he'd been given must be wrong—that surely she must be the winner—because the other woman stood apart, her stance almost disappointed at her sudden fortune.

'Closer!' Luca snapped his fingers impatiently, his eyes narrowing as he recognised one of them. The bold kitchen-hand that had approached him earlier this evening and asked to be considered for work out on the casino floor. He'd declined her instantly and if her behaviour now was anything to go by then he'd been right to do so. But who was the other woman?

Could it be her?

Shamelessly he ordered the camera to focus in on her, and his staff complied, more than used to Luca taking his rich pickings: zooming in on the prettiest girl in the room and observing her for a few moments before making his move. As if he were a lion stalking his prey, this was his domain and everyone present knew it.

It *was* her! Luca's eyes narrowed as he focussed on her image. He'd been right with his first assessment—she didn't belong in the kitchen scrubbing dishes—but neither did she belong down there being fawned and harassed, and now that she had won some money she was even more of a target. He knew how this place worked, knew that the euphoria after a win was a dangerous time, that those men would take full advantage…and it made him feel sick to the stomach.

'Who are those guys with them?' Luca asked his staff.

'Some businessmen they picked up earlier. We've been watching them for the last hour or so—they've been buying the girls drinks and now they're giving them money to play the tables—the usual.'

Which it was—this type of thing happened every hour of every day in the casino; Luca knew that more than anyone. So why, then, did he feel so disappointed? Why, then, did he feel as if he'd just been punched in the stomach?

'She paid for her own bet, though,' Dario added, listening to some information being relayed through a head piece, and, if it was seemingly a useless piece of information, it was relevant on two counts for Luca. On a professional level it made things easier for the security staff to deal with—her escort had no claim on her, there could be no pointless argument about whose money had aided the bet—but for far more personal reasons, for reasons he could barely fathom, somehow, to Luca it mattered.

It mattered a lot.

'The croupier just let us know—things are starting to get out of hand.' Dario ground out the cigar he had been smoking and focussed more cameras on the area. 'She's trying to leave, but the men insist that she stay and celebrate with them—the croupier wants the floor security to come over.'

He could sense Meg's nervousness. Those gorgeous eyes were darting, glancing around the room as if hoping to be rescued, flicking to the surveillance camera for a single second, holding his gaze without knowing it, seemingly asking him for help.

'Do it.' Luca snapped his fingers impatiently, watching on another screen as almost instantaneously the security guards made their way through the busy gaming room, the well-oiled machines of the casino moving into swift action—any potential *situation* swiftly dealt with before it escalated. Luca knew his hand-picked staff were more than capable of dealing with this, knew that in a matter of moments things would easily be brought discreetly under control and the small crowd dispersed, so why then was he pulling on his jacket, filled with something, a need almost to get out there and help her himself?

He snapped his fingers again—ordering his cheque-book and writing out a figure in his impressive violet scrawl, then stalking out of the room as his bodyguards followed without a word. They were more than used to Luca Fierezza's routine when a pretty girl won: most of her winnings would be delivered personally by cheque, so that she couldn't spend it, which got him straight to second base because it showed her he was looking out for her best interests—first base had

already been passed courtesy of his stunning good looks—
and for the final run, with the percentage of cash he handed
her, he'd invite her to join him in the high-rollers club.

Home run.

'Congratulations!'

His voice was instantly recognisable—and Meg started
in recognition as she heard it, her startled eyes swinging
round to his, actually grateful for his presence. Since her
number had come up the table had been a frenzy of activity,
everyone around her eager to celebrate, pressing her to join
in, to carry on and party into the night, when all she wanted
to do was disappear, for the glare of the spotlight to dim from
her—and now it had.

Luca was the only one who held the spotlight, the only
man in the place who could instantly regain control by his
mere presence, and regain control he did. Meg's unwelcome
companion actually melted away without even a murmur of
protest as Luca ushered Meg over to a quiet table, pouring
her a glass of water, which she accepted gratefully, before
handing her her winnings.

'Most of it is in a cheque—you can come tomorrow
morning and cash it.' He smiled at her frown. 'People often
blow their winnings, by tomorrow morning you will be more
restrained.'

'I'm more than in control now.' She gave a tight smile.
'In fact all I want to do is get the hell out of here. Is it always
so…?' She fumbled for a word for a moment and failed to
come up with one, but Luca, even with his rather more
limited disposal of the English language, found the one she
was looking for, or at least one that came close.

'Frenzied?' he offered as Meg gave a nod. 'Always.

Especially when a…' His voice trailed off as he realised somehow that she'd had an earful of shallow compliments tonight, that telling her she was beautiful was probably the last thing she wanted to hear right now. 'Join me upstairs.' He watched her eyes widen, and smiled. 'I mean, there is a quieter gaming room upstairs—a little more civilized, perhaps…' She knew where he meant—the high-rollers club. She'd seen it when she'd arrived, the elevator neatly roped off with security ensuring that only the richest and most beautiful went there, but it held little appeal for Meg.

'I'm actually really tired, but thank you for the offer,' Meg politely declined. 'I think I'll just go to bed.'

'Meg!' She hadn't realised Jasmine was standing behind her, but her indignant wail alerted Meg, followed by a very harsh whisper in her ear. 'You simply cannot turn down an invitation like that. Come on, please say yes—I don't know how to get rid of these guys!'

The same guys she's been accepting drinks and gambling chips from all night, Meg thought, but she felt herself relenting; as much as Jasmine had provoked things by accepting so much hospitality, she couldn't just turn her back on her. Maybe a quiet escape to somewhere more *civilised* would give her a chance to talk to Jasmine and tell her how precarious her situation was with those guys, and surely one drink with Luca couldn't hurt….

Who was she kidding?

The memory stick of her camera was full of photos of her travels, packed with exotic locations she'd wanted to capture for ever, but nothing came close to the man sitting opposite her at the table—whether she went for a drink or not, already his image was branded in her mind. As arrogant, as presumptuous as he'd been earlier, still she hadn't been able to shake the feeling he evoked.

'Can my friend Jasmine come?' Meg watched as his eyebrows furrowed slightly, wondered at the thought process behind the tiny gesture.

Luca didn't want her *friend* to come, didn't want the brash woman to join them—strange, he'd actually thought till now they might be sisters. They were both blond, both fairly tall, only this Jasmine was like a crude caricature of Meg. She had none of her delicacy, none of her subtle beauty and her conduct certainly wasn't befitting of the high-rollers club—yet Luca knew it was the only way he could get Meg to join him, that if he didn't act quickly, at any moment she was going to terminate the evening, so, forcing a smile, he gave a small nod.

'Of course!'

But, for once, Luca had misread a woman, because it wasn't Jasmine forcing Meg to take Luca up on his invitation, it wasn't some misguided sense of duty that had her standing up and heading towards the velvet rope that was pulled back as Luca approached.

It was something else propelling her tonight—something Meg usually chose to ignore. Whether it be hunger or emotion, it was something she usually stifled—only not tonight.

Feeling his hand on the small of her back as Luca guided her into the exclusive VIP lift, Meg acknowledged what she was feeling....

Want.

And this was a *want* she somehow couldn't deny.

Some friend, Luca thought scornfully as within seconds of arriving Jasmine disappeared into the thick fog of smoke, her inbuilt radar homing in on the richest, loudest table, and, frankly, Luca was happy to see the back of her, more than happy to turn his attention to the rather aloof woman who sat before him.

'Normally people smile when they win.'

'I was actually hoping to lose.' Meg gave a small laugh at his bemused frown. 'I wasn't particularly enjoying myself!'

'You don't like my casino?'

'No,' Meg admitted, but softened her rather brittle response with a smile. 'Though don't take it personally—I'm not really a big fan of clubs and bars, people shouting over each other just to be heard...' Conversation here was surprisingly easy. After the noise from below, the exclusive upstairs area was quieter with no gaming machines. Luca had selected a secluded area for them at a low couch well away from the tables, but it wasn't just the ambience that made talking easier—without his entourage, seated beside her, those brooding eyes and haughty features softened by the dim lighting, he was far less intimidating. In fact, after the pandemonium of before and the unwelcome company she'd been keeping, Luca Fierezza's controlled demeanour was a refreshing change—only it wasn't relaxing for Meg. Far from it!

The seedy attempts at chat-ups Meg had encountered downstairs had made her uncomfortable, ill at ease, but she didn't feel like that with Luca. Unsettled was how he made her feel. Though he hadn't lifted so much as a finger in her direction and his conversation had been supremely polite, there was definitely an awareness, a tension between them, and she knew he was biding his time, felt as if he was slowly, mentally circling her, waiting to make a move. She knew that it wasn't by accident she'd ended up at this casino magnate's table.

For the second time that night a bottle of champagne

appeared without order, only this time Meg found it easier to decline. 'I'd actually prefer some water.'

'Of course—would you like something to eat? We can—'

'I'm not hungry,' Meg interrupted quickly, but as he sent the waiter away with a flick of his wrist and proceeded to pour them both water she rather regretted her haste. Not just because she was, in fact, hungry, but because part of her wanted to stay, to linger a while longer in his presence...to simply relax and enjoy the company of this astonishingly beautiful man. Even his hands were sexy, neatly manicured fingers, olive skin contrasting with the heavy white cotton cuffs of his shirt, but Meg's forehead knitted in concentration as she glimpsed his gold cufflinks, trying to place where she'd seen the image before. Engraved on the heavy gold was the image of an orange tree surrounded by vines... She tried in vain to place them, giving in when Luca distracted her with a question.

'Are you on holiday?' Luca checked and Meg nodded.

'I'm backpacking around Europe. I've been away from home for three months.'

'And are you enjoying yourself?'

Meg hesitated a fraction too long before nodding, and Luca must have noticed the tiny pensive pause because he dismissed her enthusiastic response with an observation.

'You don't look like a backpacker.'

'What do backpackers look like?'

'Carefree,' Luca mused, 'out for fun—they certainly don't normally decline the offer of a free drink.'

'And you must know so many,' Meg responded with a heavy dash of sarcasm. Luca Fierezza's world was light years away from the one she'd inhabited these last months and she was annoyed at his assumptions—that she was some starving wretch who would jump at the chance of a free meal and an expensive drink.

He ignored her sarcasm. 'We have many backpackers that come to Niroli—some to holiday and enjoy the magnificent beaches, others for casual work.'

'It is a beautiful island,' Meg admitted. 'Well, from the little I've seen of it. I was looking forward to exploring it and…' She didn't continue, just snapped her mouth closed, realising she'd given him an opening, and Meg felt a stab of disappointment when instead of pouncing on it he instead asked a question. 'So how long do you intend to stay in Niroli?'

'I'm not sure,' Meg admitted. 'I actually came to Niroli to meet up with my brother, but there was a miscommunication. I was thinking of leaving to see if I can find work.'

'You already have a job,' Luca pointed out, for the first time acknowledging their encounter in the kitchen. 'And tomorrow you will have a better one.'

'Tomorrow I might decide to dye my hair.' Meg didn't bat an eyelid, stared coolly at him as she spoke. 'Then I won't be blond enough for you.'

'I was trying to help….' Luca attempted, but Meg shook her head at his attempt at an excuse.

'Well, you didn't,' she bristled. 'Tell me something— how come you didn't ask me to join you for dinner back in the kitchen?'

'I don't understand?'

'Oh, I think you do,' Meg said shrewdly. 'Anyway, it's irrelevant. Tomorrow, I'm going to head to Mont Avellana and look for some seasonal work.'

'Mont Avellana?' Luca sneered. 'Why would you possibly want to go there?'

'I've heard it's beautiful.'

'It is nothing compared to Niroli,' Luca derided in distaste. 'Full of gypsy *Viallis*—there is nothing for you there!'

'I'm sure they speak highly of you!' Meg made a flip comment and instantly regretted it, watching as his face darkened.

Oh, she'd read about the battle between the islands—knew that Mont Avellana was now a republic and that there was still simmering resentment between the two islands—but the way Luca was talking told Meg that this was more than just patriotism. This was hatred born from the cradle and taken to the grave. 'I'm sorry,' Meg offered, unable to comprehend that it was so, so... *personal* to Luca, but realising she had hit a raw nerve. 'I've clearly no idea what I'm talking about.'

It took a moment for him to translate her vague humour, but he accepted it with a gracious smile, swiftly changing the subject as only he could!

'Anyway—you can't go to Mont Avellana tomorrow—you are meeting with me.'

'I said no, remember.' Meg smiled, but it died on her lips as she caught his eyes. They weren't touching, a generous few inches separated them on the sofa, but she could sense his body, feel the heat of him next to her. It wouldn't have mattered where they were, whether in a busy kitchen or the luxurious surrounds of the high roller club, because again it was just the two of them—the subtle, almost indefinable process of man and woman gauging each other, that delicious heightened awareness when every move, every gesture, revealed itself in slow motion. As her tongue bobbed out to moisten her dry lips Meg knew, *knew*, he was imagining the taste of her, knew that in this volatile climate even that tiny gesture could be construed as provocative...because

it had been. He provoked her, in the most unsettling of ways.
He made her dizzy. It was as if she were riding on a carousel,
snatching images as she whirred ever faster; images not just
of the man sitting before her now, but dangerous glimpses
of where this night could lead—that full, sensual mouth
pressed onto hers, the feel of his hard, toned body pressed
against hers. Never had a man moved her so—never had she
felt such a compelling attraction to someone, never had she
been more tempted to throw caution to the wind, to let some
romance into her ordered life….

To loosen up and live a little.

Till he spoke!

'I'm sure *whatever* job you want, it can be accommodated.'

Never had she been more grateful for the dimmed lighting
as a dark, burning blush swept up her neck and over her cheeks,
her mouth dry all of a sudden, her heart hammering in her chest,
unsure if she'd misinterpreted and appalled if she hadn't—was
he offering her a job in his casino or in his bedroom?

'I speak no Italian.' Giving him the benefit of the doubt,
Meg chose her words carefully. 'I don't really see what
sort of work…'

'It doesn't have to be in the casino; perhaps you would
like to spend your time in Niroli with me?'

'With you!' She let out a shocked gasp at his directness.
'You're offering me a job as your escort!'

'Meg—' immediately he shook his head '—I think you
misunderstand. I am requesting your company for a period
of time. I would like us to have a chance to get to know each
other better. As you will understand, I'm sure, I am not permitted the luxury of casual dates—I am not able to suggest
we meet tomorrow afternoon for coffee or a chat, or a
wander on the beach—'

'Because you're too busy?' Meg interrupted scornfully. 'Too busy to deal with something as trivial as getting to know another person—oh, but if they look okay, if they can string a sentence or two together and are impressed enough by your status, then you'll simply bypass the superfluous and cut straight to the chase.'

Her angry words didn't faze him—anything but. A smile on his lips revealed very white, very even teeth. 'I think you're overreacting.'

'Do you!' Meg gave him a wide-eyed look—she really couldn't believe the audacity of him. Yes, he was stunning to look at, and, yes, she conceded, they were attracted to each other, but to have the nerve to sit there and offer to *buy* her company for a few weeks made her blood boil—that he was so pompous, so full of his self-importance to think he was *above* the social niceties, infuriated her.

'As I said, you misunderstand….'

'I don't think so.' For the first time in a long time, instead of holding it in, Meg let it out—disappointment, embarrassment all aiding her in a very few choice words. 'I'm surprised you offered dinner. Why don't we just go straight upstairs to your luxury suite?'

'Excuse me?' For the first time she startled him—a flicker of confusion in his eyes as she confronted him.

'Your luxury suite. I'm sure you've got one waiting—and given that you're clearly too busy and important for something as trivial as romance or dating, and given that I'm too tired for a late night, why don't we just go straight up there and get it over and done with?'

As his face darkened for a second Meg thought she'd gone too far—questioned the wisdom of speaking in such a manner to a man she barely knew, her feisty, sarcastic tones maybe open to misinterpretation, but as her words hit home his anger faded. The smile that had been on his lips before returned with vengeance now as he threw back his head and laughed out loud, until Meg actually managed a reluctant smile of her own.

'You are always this angry?'

'Only when I'm mistaken for a prostitute!'

'Never!' His thumb and finger found her chin, lifting her face so her eyes were level with his—touching her for the first time, the shock of contact with him tumbling her into confusion because despite her angry words before, despite the sarcasm that had laced them, she wanted him—wanted what she had moments before scorned.

Wanted him to make love to her.

'Eat with me,' Luca offered again and it was sheer self-preservation that made her shake her head, determined to politely end the conversation and just get the hell out before she did something stupid—something she would surely regret. She was here to sort her life, not complicate it further, and being a paid mistress to this man was surely a recipe for disaster!

'No.' Meg dragged the word out, jerked her chin away to break the contact as, reaching down, she picked up her bag and stood up. 'As I said, I'm very tired. Thank you for your hospitality.'

'You haven't allowed me to show you any hospitality.' He stood up as she did, clearly taken aback by her abrupt change of mood. 'But that is your choice.' He gave a brief shrug. 'I will walk you back.'

'I don't need to be walked back,' Meg declined, but Luca begged to differ.

'Your friend appears to be busy and those men are no

doubt still downstairs. It would be better if I walk you back to your room.'

If it had been anyone else offering it would have made sense. Meg had no desire to run into that group again, but neither did she want to walk with Luca. It wasn't that she didn't trust him—not for a minute did she imagine him forcing himself on her as that creepy businessman had before—but he had made his intentions exceptionally clear and so now must she.

'Thank you for the offer, Mr Fierezza, I mean, *Signor* Fierezza, but I'd prefer—'

'Luca,' he interrupted.

'I'd rather keep things formal,' Meg said crisply back, but she couldn't look at him, instead staring down at the ground, ready to turn on her heel and walk off.

'Well, in that case, my correct title is: His Royal Highness Prince Luca of Niroli.'

As her startled eyes shot up to his, despite the twist of a smile on Luca's lips at her reaction, she knew in an instant he was speaking the truth. Antoinette *hadn't* got her words mixed up, those cufflinks he was wearing, Meg realised in a flash, were actually the Niroli coat of arms she'd seen in her guide book, but it wasn't just that that convinced her, it was his sheer arrogance, the absolute confident way he carried himself—which told her he would never stoop to lying to impress a woman.

'There will be no discussion. I *will* walk you back to your room.' His hand touched her elbow and she practically shot into orbit at the contact, any argument fading on her lips as he guided her to the opening door.

'Oh, and Meg…' as the elevator glided open, as he

declined the escort from his bodyguard, Luca managed to elicit a smile from her shocked lips '…you can call me Prince for short.'

As they walked through the casino, his hand still on her elbow, Meg's mind was whirring. They made their way swiftly—he didn't need to guide her through the throng of people because they all stepped back for him, heads turning, couples nudging each other as they passed, and Meg started to understand what he had been trying to tell her. A prince couldn't date in the usual way, couldn't walk into a bar unrecognised or linger over a coffee as he got to know a virtual stranger, and those thoughts were confirmed when finally they left the crowds behind and walked the long corridor to her room.

'You didn't know?'

'No,' Meg admitted. "Antoinette, the kitchen hand, did say something, but I thought she was…' She gave a helpless shrug. 'Shouldn't you be locked away in a palace or something, with bodyguards protecting you?'

'I should be according to my grandfather—the king,' he added as Meg blew a breath skywards, the entire conversation so bizarre she couldn't believe it was taking place. 'But it is not how I choose to live; I like to work—to run my businesses. Here I get a shot of a normal life.'

'Normal!' Meg gave a wry grin. 'Even before I heard your title, Luca, you didn't fit into that description.'

'I have a comfortable life—but I work hard for it. Yes, I can afford many things, and maybe I could just live off my title, but I still take pride in my work, my business ventures—that is why I mainly choose not to use my title, why here I prefer to be called just Luca, though naturally most people know who I am.'

They were at her door now and Meg wished they weren't, wished somehow she were staying in some remote cottage at the end of a very long beach, instead of a shared room a mere ten minutes away…

She didn't want the night to end—even though she'd terminated it, now she wanted to prolong it and it had nothing to do with his royal title, more the fascinating man behind it, the man she was starting to glimpse.

'Thank you,' Meg said simply.

'For what?'

'For coming over when you did. Things could have got out of hand otherwise.'

'You have to be careful, Meg. Your friend is not much of an escort for you.'

'I don't need an escort,' Meg answered stoutly, but Luca remained unmoved, shaking his head at her proud words.

'Tonight things could have been very different—I see a lot of things that go on. Buy your own drinks, Meg, and hold onto your glass. Don't let it out of your sight.'

'You sound like my father.' Meg rolled her eyes as she chatted. 'When I say my father, I mean my adopted father. I had all the lectures before I set off on my trip—'

Her voice halted abruptly; she was stunned at her own words, at how easily she'd revealed a piece of herself to Luca. She'd been with Jasmine for weeks yet she had never revealed this, yet here she was, an hour into Luca's company, and she was opening up like a flower in the sun with him. But Luca didn't seem to notice the revelation, just carried on the conversation where she had so hastily left it.

'I would not like to be your father.' He gave a wry smile. 'I am sure the man must never rest, worrying about his beautiful daughter.' He'd called her beautiful and instead of flinching or refusing to take the compliment she absorbed it, even felt a little bit beautiful. Luca stared thoughtfully back at her. 'You're not going to come tomorrow?' When she shook her head he pushed for a reason. 'Can I ask why?'

She paused for a moment before answering, wondered how on earth she could explain that, though she wanted to, though she was more attracted to him than she'd ever been to *anyone*, it was just too dangerous, too damned scary to let him into her life. 'I don't want to complicate my life; the reason I'm travelling is that I'm actually trying to sort a few things out….' Meg answered as honestly as she could without telling him her painful truth. 'And, somehow, I don't think spending time with you is going to help me achieve that.'

'It might.'

'I doubt it.' Meg gave a rueful smile. How could a holiday romance with a royal prince possibly help her find the peace she craved? But never had she been more tempted to relent, the rigid self-discipline she usually lived by treacherously displaced by his presence. 'It's been nice meeting you, Luca.'

'May I kiss you *goodbye?*'

She'd been about to shake her head, to refuse his request for a kiss goodnight, but his choice of words had her hesitating.

It really *was* goodbye.

A chance encounter that would never in her life be repeated—men like Luca didn't come around twice in a lifetime—and Meg bit down on her lip, torn between fear and want, sensing the danger yet lusciously curious.

'I don't think that's a very good idea,' Meg breathed, her hormones weeping in protest as she denied them the goodies that were clearly on offer as her mind scrambled to regain control. 'Anyway, I thought it was supposed to be the other way around.' He was watching her mouth as she spoke, as she attempted a joke, attempted to delay the inevitable. 'We're supposed to kiss and *then* you turn into a prince!'

'For you, maybe there is better.' His hand was on her cheek, his thumb playing with her lower lip. 'You *deserve* better,' Luca elaborated. 'Maybe your kiss would make me a king.'

She didn't know if he was joking, didn't know if it was just a light-hearted response, and frankly she didn't care— Luca was as skilled at flirting as he was at manipulating. His mouth was just inches away, teasing her with his breath as he spoke, honing in on her distraction, asking for something only moments ago she wouldn't have considered.

'Don't go to Mont Avellana tomorrow—spend the day with me instead.'

Breathless, dizzy and deliciously disorientated, she struggled with what now seemed a straightforward question, her mind trying to recall the reasons she should decline.

'The day?'

'I'll show you Niroli—and maybe then you'll decide to stay on for a while, maybe you can find the peace you crave here.'

She opened her mouth to protest, to remind him why she couldn't stay, but with a few words Luca had made the impossible suddenly feasible. Taking a strand of hair, he brushed it behind her ear, all the while staring into her eyes. 'We are two very different people but with one constant.' He didn't need to elaborate, their arousal, their attraction achingly evident, but Luca broke the contact, stepped back into the hallway and asked her a very pertinent question. 'Did refusing my kiss give you peace?'

She didn't say anything but Meg's answer was obvious, her whole body screaming a protest at Luca's rapid withdrawal.

'I will be in the foyer tomorrow at nine.'

He walked away then—Luca's bid clearly in, leaving it

for Meg to decide. He didn't even offer a backward glance as he walked back along the corridor, leaving Meg jumbled and confused, fumbling in her bag for her keys, then entering her room and sitting on the bed, somehow trying to make sense of all that had occurred.

They couldn't last.

That much Meg understood.

But they couldn't end yet either, Meg realised; the attraction was too strong, the emotion too intense to just walk away.

Pulling out her purse, Meg slid her fingers into the wallet and pulled out a well-worn picture, one she hadn't looked at in weeks, but occasionally, at times like this, when decisions needed to be made, it was called upon. Even though she'd seen it a thousand times, even though she'd *lived* it, still the image shocked her.

Pained eyes in a gaunt face stared back at Meg, her skeletal frame engulfed by a wheelchair, a nurse at her side holding her hand as she struggled to come up from her lowest point.

There were a million reasons to set her alarm for six and get the hell out of Niroli, to organise her backpack and literally run for the hills.

But there was one very good reason to stay. Falling asleep with the photo still in her hand, Meg was only vaguely aware of Jasmine bumping around in the night, her mind focussed on one thought only.

Tonight, for the first time in her life, and only with Luca, she'd actually felt beautiful.

CHAPTER FIVE

'I'M GLAD YOU decided to stay.'

As Luca joined her in the crowded foyer, Meg was glad she'd decided to stay too. The hour between waking and seeing him had plagued Meg with doubt and indecision. She was almost sure that her vision of the man she had met last night wouldn't stand up to the scrutiny of the morning glare, that somehow seeing him again could only taint the delicious memory.

Wrong.

If anything, Luca was more stunning.

Dressed casually in dark denim jeans and a black T-shirt, unshaven and unkempt, he looked even more ravishing, but there was no time for awkward small talk, no time for anything at all really, as Luca took her by her arm and shepherded her out the foyer and straight into the luxurious confines of a sleek silver sports car.

'I thought today was supposed to be relaxing!' Meg attempted as the car sped away from the casino.

'Now, it will be,' Luca said cryptically, glancing in the rear-view mirror and finally slowing down. 'I'll ring Luigi now and tell him I haven't been kidnapped.'

'Your bodyguard?' Meg checked as Luca nodded and

punched in speed-dial. Even if her Italian was extremely limited, it soon became clear that Luigi was less than impressed at his boss's hasty exit.

'Sorry about that.' Luca grinned when the call ended. 'Luigi is supposed to accompany me whenever I go outside the casino or palace. I do not like it.'

'I wouldn't either.' Meg smiled, glancing shyly over to him. 'I'm glad it's just us.'

'Me too.' Luca nodded. 'You look wonderful!'

'Er, I doubt it.' Meg grimaced. Never had her backpack's offerings appeared more measly. She'd been hoping to spend yesterday getting acquainted with a washing machine, but for the biggest date of her life she'd been left with no choice other than faded denim shorts and a pale lemon halter-neck. Still, given it was Luca, she'd bypassed her runners for some gorgeous leather sandals she'd purchased in Rome, and instead of scraping her hair back into its usual sightseeing fare of a pony-tail had blow-dried it and left it down. 'I wasn't exactly inundated with choice.'

'Inundated?' Luca checked.

'Spoilt…' Meg attempted to no avail. 'I don't have many clothes to choose from—I've tried to pack something for most eventualities, but a day trip with royalty wasn't something I'd planned on!'

'We may not get into the restaurant I wanted to go to for lunch—I don't think they allow shorts…' Luca shrugged '…but that's no problem.'

'Sorry.' Meg flinched.

'I tease you.' Luca laughed. 'There are some perks to being a prince—you could be wearing nothing more than a bikini and we would get the best table. I meant what I said—you look wonderful.'

She did.

Luca, too, had been wondering what to expect this morning. So many times before the raw beauty he'd witnessed in a woman had disappeared the second she'd found out *who* he was—commandeering the salon, spending up in the boutique. He'd almost resigned himself to greeting a stranger this morning, yet here she was, more beautiful, more vibrant, more sexy than the woman he had met last night—acres of soft, browned skin on show, her hair a blond fragrant cloud, and just a slick of gloss on those incredibly kissable lips....

'Where are we going?'

'Does it matter?'

Turning his attention from the road for a second, he held her gaze and Meg bit down on her lip, processing his question for a moment before answering, her single-word answer the boldest thing she'd ever said.

'No.'

In fact, if they never set foot out of the car, Meg wouldn't have minded. Dressed more casually, and well away from the extravagance and decadence of the casino, Luca was infinitely more relaxed, his company engaging. But Luca actually did have plans for the day. He wanted to show her all that Niroli had to offer and show her he did, gliding the sleek car through the steep hills, at every turn the view even more stunning.

'No more!' Luca grinned when Meg begged him to stop for yet another photo shoot. 'Or you will run out of space— wait till we get to the ruins. We stop now at one of the wineries and I'll ask them to make us a picnic.'

Which, when it was Luca Fierezza asking, meant that a blanket was included, the hamper groaning under the weight of Niroli delicacies, and Meg wanted to taste them all, only not just yet—first they spent a sun-drenched day exploring. Luca steered them well away from the usual tourist haunts in the south of the island and instead headed north where he showed her the ancient Roman ruins, regaling her with tale after tale, making her privy to information that could never be gleaned from a history book. But as excellent a tourist guide as he made, as much as he seemed to enjoy showing her Niroli, the day was about them—the sultry air thicker somehow when blended with desire, awareness thrumming as they explored, not just the temple and amphitheatre, but each other's minds. And by the time Luca spread out the blanket and they shared their picnic, Meg knew a single day could never be enough to scratch the surface of all it had to offer—only she wasn't thinking about Niroli!

'Here,' Luca said proudly, pouring her an icy glass of champagne as she gazed around the amphitheatre. 'There are often concerts held here—there will be one this weekend….'

'For the Feast?'

'You have heard about it?'

'One of the shopkeepers told me.' Meg gave an abstracted nod, biting into slivers of bitter orange dipped in dark chocolate and closing her eyes as she relished the taste. 'This,' she declared, 'is the nicest thing I've ever tasted.'

'You said that about the olive dip, and then the cannoli. It is good to see someone who likes their food.' Luca frowned at her reaction. 'Why does that make you laugh?'

'It just does.' Meg's answer was evasive, a first date not really the best time to slip in the little gem of the eating disorder that had ruled her for years, but, closing her eyes, Meg lay back and smiled as the warm sun bathed her, relishing the moment, his casual observation a revelation. Here, away from it all, for the first time in the longest time, she'd actually forgotten her problem, *had* just enjoyed food as it should be enjoyed. Oh, she was long past the frantic calorie counts, way, way past controlling every morsel she consumed, but to simply *enjoy*… Luca could never have even hazarded a guess as to how much this moment meant to her.

'You are having a good time?' Luca enquired, lying down on the blanket beside her, his body just inches away, so achingly close all Meg wanted to do was reach over and touch him. She could feel the hum of sexual energy between them, his masculinity bathing her now, only with more ferocity than the sun, her skin tingling as even with her eyes still closed she could feel him watching her.

'It's been great.'

'It has…' Luca let out a long sigh, his body so close she could feel his chest move beside her. 'It is nice to relax.'

'I don't suppose you get much chance,' Meg offered. 'What with work and…' She gave a tiny frown, peeped her eyes open to look at him. 'Do you have to do all the ceremonial, well…stuff?' She gave a helpless shrug but thankfully Luca understood.

'Always there are commitments. Take this weekend— there will be many events I have to attend as a royal prince.'

'You don't sound as if you want to?'

'It is not about want, it is about duty,' Luca explained. 'It is what is expected of me—and lately…' He didn't finish, just shook his head, but Meg's curiosity was piqued now.

'Lately?' she pushed.

'You ask too many questions. It is not correct.'

'Excuse me?' Meg's eyes were wide open now as Luca attempted to put her in her place.

'You should not pry so much. I will tell you what you need to know.'

'I don't *need* to know anything.' Meg gave a shocked laugh. 'I was asking because I *wanted* to know. And don't pull rank on me when it suits!'

'It is not about pulling rank—when you are out with royalty—'

'But I'm not,' Meg broke in, disarming his rather terse response with a smile. 'I'm out with Luca—remember? That was the reason you left Luigi behind, that was the whole point of today—to get to know each other a bit better away from it all.'

'Are you always this argumentative?'

'Always.' Meg smiled as Luca's face blackened. 'Now, if there's something you'd prefer not to discuss, then you just have to say so, but, please, don't hide behind your title!'

Closing her eyes, she lay her head back down and even though her heart was hammering in her chest at the small confrontation, she certainly wasn't about to let him know that. If Luca thought he could talk to her like that, then he'd better do a quick rethink! And, Meg decided, if he didn't break the angry silence, then she certainly wouldn't—she'd start snoring if she had to!

'When I was younger I…' as Luca conceded, as he struggled to find the right word, Meg felt her heart soar as she opened her eyes and looked over to him '…was a little wild.'

'A little?' Meg checked.

'A lot,' Luca admitted. 'Always I was in trouble. Now I stay out of trouble, but the king has a long memory and so do the people of Niroli. He spoke to me recently—told me I have to…' He gave a frustrated shrug. 'Now, I prefer not to discuss family business.'

'Fine.' Meg smiled. 'That's all you had to say.'

'So, now it is my turn—why did you come?'

'Because you asked me to.'

'Not here.' Luca shook his head. 'Why did you choose to travel? You said you were here to sort things out. Can I ask what?'

And maybe this was one first date where she could reveal, because, in that second, it didn't feel as if they'd only just met. Her eyes were looking straight into his, the sun blocked out by his presence, it didn't feel as if there were a million barriers between them—it felt as if they were one, as if she were looking at a man she'd always known, just hadn't really met yet.

'What?' Luca pushed, just a touch too soon, the brave leap she was about to take thwarted by impatience, and Meg recoiled back into herself, shaking her head as if to clear it, stunned at how close she had come to letting him in—letting *anyone* in.

'I'd prefer not to say.'

'You confuse me, Meg. One minute you are so strong, so sure, yet the next…' He gave a helpless shrug. 'You are very complicated, yes?'

'Yes.'

It wasn't the answer he was expecting, perhaps a small admission, a revelation, but when there was none forthcoming Luca, surprisingly, graciously conceded. 'Perhaps we need to get to know each other even better,' Luca suggested. 'Maybe one day isn't enough for us?'

'Maybe,' Meg gulped.

'So…' his voice was slow and measured, cautious this time as he approached '…will you stay a little longer? More than just this day?' His face was moving in closer as she toyed with her answer, but he didn't wait to hear it. 'Maybe this will help you decide.'

She'd been so sure he was about to kiss her, so absolutely

sure, it was *all* she could think about, so when his hand lightly dusted her stomach, when his warm fingers brushed the gap between her shorts and top, her body tightened in delicious confusion. Meg could almost hear the reverse sirens sounding in her brain as it instructed her neural pathways to move their guard, that she was being attacked from a different angle, but even as her stomach tightened in reflex Luca changed tack, his mouth moving in, and Meg closed her eyes as his hand snaked around the back of her head. He moved a fraction closer, his breath warm on her cheekbone, making her wait, her lips twitching in nervous expectation, anticipating the feel of his mouth on hers, her breath held in her lungs as so slowly he moved in, but nothing in her imagination could ever rival the true feel of him, the heat of his mouth when it met hers. Like a reflex action her lips parted, his kiss as direct as his approach to her had been, his tongue sliding in offering a simultaneous taste of champagne and power.

Such power, his kiss utterly potent, making mockery of any past efforts, turning the few men she had dated into mere boys as his skilled mouth searched hers and his arms wrapped fiercely around her body. For ever he kissed her, drenching her with his passion, banishing reticence, pressing himself so hard against her it was as if they were one person, his lips first paying her mouth the most thorough of attention, then blazing a trail down her neck, kissing her exposed shoulder deeply, his tongue moving up to the base of her neck and then back again. It was to die for, so erotic, so, so shatteringly sexy Meg had to remind herself to breathe.

As Luca's hand cupped her bottom he pressed her heated groin into him, his erection wedged against her. It was Meg kissing him now, hungry lips meeting his scented neck, tasting

Luca's warm flesh as her fingers knotted in his hair—the salt of his skin on her tongue, his cologne filling her nostrils as his other hand moved to the front, the pad of his thumb plying her swollen nipple through her top. With each measured move he spun her ever faster, whirring her mind, her body, into one giddy blur—his hands touching her where her body needed it, *before* Meg even *knew* it herself. How easy it would be to just let go, to give in and follow to where he was taking her, to let this vortex consume her, but so ingrained was her control, so fearful was she of losing it, that with supreme effort Meg pulled back, the ground coming up to meet her as she jumped off at the last moment, staring at him with stunned, fearful eyes as the world carried on spinning.

'We can't!' The words she gasped out were more directed at herself than Luca; she was stunned at what had just taken place, at her body's perilous response to him, but Luca's reply just confused her further.

'We won't,' he murmured, moving in, kissing her again, only more tenderly now. 'We wouldn't,' he said between breathless mouthfuls. 'Not here…not somewhere so public. Now, we just kiss.'

Just kiss!

His comfort offered no solace. If, for Luca, that was just a kiss, then what would it be like to be made love to by him, if that was what he could do to her with his mouth…? Meg's mind begged quiet, needed him to stop, her ingrained restraint so violently compromised it actually scared her.

'Please, Luca…'

Something in her voice reached him, his mouth stilling, those black eyes surprisingly tender as he stared down at her.

'I have upset you?'

'No…' She was biting down on her lip in an effort to stop

crying, every emotion she'd ever suppressed clamouring for freedom as somehow Luca unleashed her. 'It's just too soon…' Her eyes pleaded with him for understanding, for Luca to realise that it wasn't sex she was talking about here. 'It's too soon to be feeling like *this!*'

'Then stay,' Luca said simply, holding her in his arms, only more tenderly now, letting her catch her breath as everything calmed down. As the world came back into focus, almost the same as when she'd left it…only somehow different now.

'Now, I'll take you to the beach.' After a few moments in Luca's arms, when still Meg hadn't responded to his suggestion, Luca decided on a change of scene and Meg was surprised how relieved she felt that their date wasn't over yet. But, as nice as he could be when he remembered, as engaging and charming as he was without even trying, every now and then Meg was reminded of his station in life—Luca Fierezza was so thoroughly spoiled, so impossibly arrogant at times, sometimes Meg honestly thought he was joking.

He wasn't!

'Niroli has the most beautiful beaches,' Luca elaborated, offering his hand to help her up.

'I don't have my bathers with me.'

'Bathers?'

'A swimming costume,' Meg attempted, but Luca screwed up his nose at the Australianism.

'They are horrible words—I like women to wear bikinis! Come,' he said impatiently as Meg started to clear up the picnic. 'Just leave it.'

'You can't just leave it! What about the blanket, the basket…?' Meg insisted, but Luca had other ideas, striding off towards the car and clearly expecting her to follow.

'If they want it, then they can come and find it!'

'What's wrong?' As Meg climbed into the car, almost immediately she realised something was up, Luca frowning into the phone as he checked his messages.

'I'm not sure,' was Luca's distracted reply, his face rigid as he replayed his voicemail message, before finally he turned around and faced her. 'I have to go back to the casino. It would appear I am needed.'

'That's fine.' So riddled with doubt was Meg, she was sure he was making it up, sure that her little exposé before must have put him off, but, forcing a smile, she tried not to let her disappointment show as they drove towards the casino in silence. When he didn't elaborate further, didn't suggest that they meet up later, Meg could sit on her hands no longer.

'Luca.' Taking a deep breath, Meg decided to bite the bullet, almost managed to convince herself that she was imagining the sudden tension between them. It was only since the phone call the mood had changed—maybe he was worried about work. 'Tomorrow, why don't we—?'

'Let's just wait and see, shall we?' Luca snapped out his response, lifted his hand from the steering wheel and flicked away her attempt. For Meg it was like being slapped, her face burning as he declined her brave offer, her voice when it came again as tense and as strained as the expression he was wearing.

'Would you be able to drop me off at one of the beaches…?' She didn't even get to finish, Luca flicking on the indicator and pulling over before the sentence was even over, and for Meg it was the final straw, everything that had been before evaporated into thin air as she opened the passenger door and stepped out, the atmosphere so suddenly vile, she didn't even bother to say goodbye….

And neither did Luca.

CHAPTER SIX

'YOU'RE SURE?' A muscle was pounding in Luca's cheek as Dario fiddled with buttons and the grainy CCTV footage came up on the screen.

'Here we see the girls looking at the jewellery, now she is handling it—the staff kept a close eye on them, of course.' Luca didn't say anything, his black eyes narrowing, watching as Meg held the earrings in her hand, then handed them to her friend, who held them up to her a moment before handing them back to the assistant. 'Here, four hours later, the footage isn't as good—the main camera was on the front desk—but you see she came back with the man she had been drinking with in the gaming room and asked to see the jewels again. This is when the man she was with suddenly collapsed.'

Luca snarled. 'It was a distraction technique; a ruse to keep the main camera on the front desk and distract the staff.'

'*No.*' Dario shook his head, extremely experienced in all aspects of casino security; he was one of the few people who could disagree with Luca and get away with it. 'I also thought it might be a distraction technique, but I have checked with the hospital—he is in the coronary care unit after suffering a major heart attack.' The security chief's words were delivered in rapid Italian, but his voice was nonchalant—theft was a common occurrence in the casino, but with the security so tight it was quickly and easily dealt with. 'Here you see her more clearly now. I don't think she planned it, just saw the opportunity and got greedy.'

Even though he'd been told the facts, even though Dario rarely made a mistake, still he hoped it would be Jasmine that would appear on screen, that somehow Dario had mixed up the two women, but despite the grainy footage, even if Meg's face never fully came into view, there was no mistaking the unique, stunning top she had worn last night. Luca sucked in a deep breath, his teeth gritting together. What the hell did she have to go and do that for? He'd have given her anything she wanted, anything at all. Hell, he'd been so smitten, if she'd wanted some damn jewellery he'd have bought it for her without batting an eye, and now here she was, a woman he'd actually thought different, a woman he'd respected, showing her true colours—stealing his own family jewels.

It made him sick—sick to the stomach, yet he was also filled with a strange, hollow sadness, not just for what he had lost, but because he knew what he had to do. There was a strict one-strike policy at the casino, with no exceptions—even if he had thought for a short while that this Meg was one.

'You've spoken to the friend?'

'When we searched the room. Apparently Miss Donovan was in and out last night.' Dario gave a shrug. 'The jewels were wrapped up in the top Miss Donovan was wearing and had been stuffed in the backpack—we've got all the evidence we need to call the police.'

Luca stared at the frozen image on the screen, trying to relate the deceitful, shady character to the woman he thought he had glimpsed, the woman he had held in his arms and kissed, the proud, dignified woman he had wanted to get to know.

The woman who had duped him.

'Do it, then.' Luca stared one more time at the image frozen on the screen, then gave a terse nod as, on his command, Dario picked up the telephone. 'Tell the police you will let them know when she returns to the casino.' It was said entirely without feeling, his orders exactly as they would be for any other common thief who attempted to get one over on Luca Fierezza, but if Dario had looked up as Luca stalked towards the door he might have noticed the rigid shoulders and bunched fists as his boss made to leave the room. He *did* look up, though, as Luca turned and gave one unusual final instruction. 'Page me when she arrives—this I want to see.'

Luca was used to burying himself in work, the casino just one of his many business ventures, each one demanding scrupulous attention to detail, ruthlessness and resolute indifference, so why couldn't he concentrate? Why was it that, over and over, he kept staring at his phone, checking his pager?

'Concentrarsi'. He snapped the order to himself, answered a red-flagged email, and with a few strokes of the keyboard gave the order to fire one of his CEOs in the UK as well as ordering an internal audit on one of his growing business ventures on the Gold Coast in Australia....

Where Meg was from....

What was it with her? *Dio!* She wasn't the first woman he'd met who'd shown her true colours and it certainly wasn't the first time he'd had to have someone arrested, so why, no matter how hard he tried not to think about her, did every road, every thought he had lead to Meg?

Burying his head in his hands, Luca sucked in air and, closing his eyes, he gave into a rare moment of introspection.

She wasn't the problem, Luca decided; it was the rather confronting talk he'd had with his grandfather, King Giorgio, just a few days before that was making her attractive—making this thief who came in the night the ultimate forbidden fruit.

"Stay out of trouble, Luca.' The king's voice, though weak from his declining health, hadn't wavered as he'd delivered his order for Luca to keep his nose clean—to stand up and face the fact that he was a potential heir to the Niroli throne.

And though he'd been born a prince, though technically the chance he might one day rule Niroli had been explained to him as he'd grown up, deep down it had never really seemed plausible. Two years ago he'd been way down in line to the throne—the king had had, as the saying went, an heir and a spare: his first-born son, Antonio, and then Luca's father, Paulo, and any possibility of one day ruling Niroli had seemed far away in the distance.

Then the accident had happened.

Two years ago the royal house of Niroli had been thrown into turmoil when a boating accident had claimed the life of the immediate heirs. Antonio and his wife Francesca, along with Luca's father, Paulo, had been tragically killed. While any family would have struggled to come to terms with such loss, for a royal family it threw up more issues, which, with each passing day, were becoming more pressing.

Since the accident, King Giorgio's health had deteriorated rapidly—a proud man, he did not want to rule from his sickbed and was determined to provide his people with a fitting heir before his abdication. The people of Niroli had mourned along with the royal family, had suffered with them through the bad times, and now it was time to pave way for the new. Summoning the family members from around the globe, the king had informed them of his plans to find Niroli's new ruler from amongst them—one in keeping with The Rules, a strict set of orders that the ruler must live by.

Raking his hands through his jet-black hair, Luca tried and failed to imagine himself as King.

He loved his country.

He'd die for his county—and that wasn't an idle statement: the neighbouring island of Mont Avellana had once been under Niroli's rule, but after a bitter battle, control had been lost and it had become a republic. Even today, there was still rivalry and resentment. Unlike the extinct volcanoes that existed on Niroli, there were grumblings of discord that could spill over at any given time—and Luca knew, without a flicker of doubt, he'd be in the front line if he was called.

Yes, Luca sighed, he'd die for his country, but could he live for it?

Live only for it?

'No more scandal, Luca.' The king had waved a thin, gnarled finger at him—that one gesture, that short sentence, summing up a colourful life. Luca's teenage years had been mired in petty crime and scandal not befitting a royal prince; it was a life the tabloids had gleefully dissected over the years and like vultures still they wanted more scandal— scandal that somehow Luca had always provided. 'Niroli has given you a good life—fast cars, beautiful women—and over and over our beloved people have forgiven your mistakes, always loved you, so now it is time for you to pay your debt, to put that life behind you once and for all. Now is the time for you to maybe become more than a man—you are in the running to be King. So, think of settling down, winding down your business interests and keeping more suitable company. You owe it not just to me, but to our people, to stay out of trouble, Luca, to give them something back, something they can enjoy—a wedding, perhaps!'

'You're telling me to marry?' Luca couldn't believe what he was hearing—couldn't believe what was being asked of him—but the king had stood his ground.

'I'm telling you that your reckless days are over—that a suitable bride might prove a better escort than some of the women you choose to date. The people of Niroli need to see that you have grown up and a good wife would be a fitting gesture.' As Luca had opened his mouth to put his point the king overrode him, his frail voice gaining momentum, reminding Luca, even if he didn't need it, that this wasn't a grandfatherly chat—Giorgio was, for now, still King! 'I am not asking you, Luca, I am ordering you. I do not want to open a newspaper again and see a slur with your name attached to it. Those days are gone—for ever!'

Staring blindly out at his luxurious office, the king's words still buzzing in his ears, Luca felt the prison gates slowly closing behind him. He glimpsed a future he couldn't fathom: his business interests slowly wound down to accommodate a more royal schedule; performing his duties with a beautiful nameless face on his arm. A privileged lifestyle many would hanker for, but for Luca it felt as if he were about to be delivered a life sentence.

'You were born for this,' Luca said sharply to himself, heaving aside his doubts, forcing himself out of his introspection and facing facts. He couldn't help Meg—even if he wanted to, his hands were tied. It wasn't just the king who had spoken, but history itself! As if the first of The Rules of the Royal House of Niroli had been decreed with him in mind:

*The ruler of Niroli must be a moral leader for the
people and is bound to keep order in the Royal House.
Any act that brings the monarchy into disrepute
through immoral conduct or criminal activity will rule
a contender out of the succession to the throne.*

There were ten rules the leader of Niroli must abide by,
but this was the first—and this was the one that Luca had
failed on many occasions. His playboy reputation was leg-
endary on the island, and back when he was a teenager he'd
had a few run-ins with the police himself, arrested for petty
theft and several other misdemeanours. And though charges
had never been laid, and technically there was no criminal
record—the people of Niroli's memories were long. As the
king had pointed out, Niroli had been more than good to him
and now they needed a leader.

Now it was Luca's time to abide by the rules.

Meg was on her own.

So why, instead of turning off his pager and getting back
to work, did he jump when it bleeped? Why, when he was
informed by Dario that Meg was approaching the casino, did
he head down towards the entrance?

Why did this woman still move him so?

'Signorina Donovan?'

So deep in her own thoughts was Meg as she wandered
back from the beach that the police cars screeching along-
side, lights and sirens blazing, at first jolted rather than
alarmed her. She was sure there must have been an accident,
an incident taking place perhaps, certainly something that
didn't concern her—until they said her name….

'Alex?' It was her first thought. The most reliable, trustworthy man she knew hadn't turned up yesterday and now the police were calling her by name. Meg's heart lurched with all the fear of the innocent—something terrible must have happened to Alex. 'Is he okay?'

But her question was never answered, instead she was shoved against a wall, her head hitting the rough stone. Pain coursed through her. Merciless hands ruthlessly searched her, groping her, pressing against her shorts, shamelessly lingering a little too long over her flimsy top, and Meg felt her fear, her panic, subside into revulsion…into dread.

'Get off!' Pale lips attempted to get the words out, blood was trickling down from her head. 'Get your hands off me…' But it was like being trapped in a nightmare, her mouth forming the words, her brain screaming them, only no sound was coming out, like some horror movie on mute. She could feel inappropriate hands still groping her, still touching her, still *violating* her as people gathered and watched. She could smell the stale breath of the police officer as the crowd called out insults in Italian.

'Don't!' It was all she could manage, the one word that did come out, her slender hand clasping the fat, podgy fingers as they slid up her thigh, her lips snarling in disgust, distaste as she saw his leer, the beads of sweat on his upper lip. Meg decided she wouldn't give him the satisfaction of her fear, wouldn't give the gathering crowd the show they so clearly desired by fighting with this brute. Instead she stopped struggling, just leant against the wall with her eyes closed till it was over, till she felt the cool of the handcuffs as they were snapped on her wrists and she was unceremoniously spun around and marched towards one of the waiting police cars. The ideal world she had so briefly glimpsed just a few hours ago was suddenly frightening and confusing.

First Luca's brutal rejection, now flashing lights and sirens and jeers from the crowd, but she refused to cry, refused to let anyone see how much this was hurting her, refused to look at anyone—until her eyes caught sight of him….

Luca Fierezza standing there, despite the forty-degree heat, impassive and cool, watching the proceedings from a slight distance, his face unreadable as he registered her plight. Meg's first instinct was to cry out to him, to ask him for assistance. She knew somehow that he was the one person who could help her, but even as she opened her mouth to call out to him she choked her plea back. The black eyes staring at her held none of the warmth she had briefly witnessed, the mouth that had kissed her was now pressed in the same firm, grim line it had been when she'd left him, and somewhere deep inside Meg knew, just *knew* this was his doing, knew in that instant that he wasn't going to help her.

Well, she wouldn't let him see her pain—wouldn't let him know any of her agony. Whatever twisted game he was playing, she wasn't going to partake in it! And though the fight in her might have appeared to have died—her body seemingly weak and pliable as the police officers roughly shepherded her into one of the cars—inside she was regrouping, stronger perhaps than she had ever been in her life. Pressed against the door, she pulled her thighs away so there was no contact with her captor, closed her mind to his angry words. Meg hunched herself forward, watched as blood dripped from her face to her legs, and ran a dry tongue over her bruised and swollen mouth. Taking slow, deep breaths as the car careered through Niroli at breakneck speed, she tried to somehow regain control when there appeared to be none.

She would call the embassy—whatever mess she was in it would soon be sorted. There were rules for this sort of thing, procedures in place for tourists in trouble abroad—she had nothing to fear.

Despite the direness of her predicament, Meg felt her fear abate a notch, the steely grit that had got her through her difficult, difficult life coming to the fore when she needed it most, but it wavered a touch as she recalled Luca's hostile stare—the man she had almost trusted, nearly let into her life, causing her more pain than the injuries and indignity she had so recently suffered.

Well, she'd learnt her lesson.

For the first time she'd let down her guard, trusted that the world could be kind and gentle if only she let it, and look what had happened....

Never again.

Meg held her head high now, stared out of the window as they turned a corner and the Niroli palace came into view, its impressive walls burnt orange in the late afternoon sun, its beauty mocking her as the car halted and she was roughly pulled out, the sight of the palace her last image of the outside world as she was frogmarched into the police station and forced to endure another degrading search before she was bundled into a tiny, dimly lit cell.

No one would hurt her again.

CHAPTER SEVEN

SHE DESERVED IT.

Scribbling his signature on a thick pile of correspondence, Luca tried and failed to put the image of Meg from his mind. Since her arrest, Luca had made several impromptu checks on various areas of the casino, taken care of endless phone calls he'd long been putting off, and, for the first time since he'd taken the business over, cleared his overflowing correspondence tray, but nothing he did managed to fully erase the image of Meg's stricken face as the police had led her to the car.

Where had he seen that expression before? His mind started to drift, to search the recesses of his mind in an attempt to match the image he was seeking, but Luca abruptly halted it there.

Forget about her, Luca demanded of himself. Forget about the wretched thief, the woman who could have brought him shame and scandal when he needed it the least. Glancing at his watch, Luca saw that it was nearly midnight. Glad that this vile day was nearly over and with a shake of his head, he stood up, deciding to head to his suite and shower and change, then head to the bar, end his wretchedness with a stiff drink and perhaps some company. Only despite his best efforts, still Luca's thoughts reluctantly turned to her....

She hadn't even put up a fight, Luca scorned—if she'd been innocent, surely she'd have been enraged, hissing and spitting like a kitten. No, it was almost as if she'd been expecting it, had *known* what the police were there for.

'A call for you, sir.' Despite the lateness of the hour, his secretary buzzed the intercom—her day not over until Luca discharged her.

'No more calls,' Luca snapped. 'I'm finished for the day—you can go home now.'

'It's Her Royal Highness.'

And if it had been any other minute of any other day, Luca would have taken the call without hesitation, his mother, Laura, the one woman whose calls weren't screened, who was usually put through without hesitation—just not this time.

'I said no calls,' Luca barked. But instead of marching out of the office, instead of heading to the bar where it would be so, so much safer to go, he sat back down in the darkness, black bile churning in his stomach as a piece of this reluctant puzzle slotted into place....

Unwelcome, seldom-visited memories pelted his mind like a sudden hailstorm—a storm so violent, so forceful, so rapid in its arrival that there was no time to seek cover, no time to shield himself from its onslaught, so that all he could do was wait, sit at his desk with his head in his hands and ride out the storm in the hope it would quickly pass.

It didn't.

Each memory lashed him more fiercely.

Watching again his father's fist slam into his mother's face, her long black hair, taut in his fingers, as over and over she took the beating, never once crying out—just as Luca hadn't.

Peering into the room that hateful night he had stifled his screams by instinct, something telling him, even at this tender age, that what he was witnessing must never be acknowledged.

He'd tried, though. Ramming his knuckles into his fist, Luca felt the slap of his mother's hand again on his cheek; felt the confusion, the bewilderment all over again as she'd later denied what he had seen take place, told him off for even *thinking* such filthy things.

But he *had* seen it, had seen his mother, despite the indignity, somehow still proud, somehow stronger in her passiveness than the brute that beat her.

He'd seen that expression once in his mother, her face etched with stricken dignity as that bastard had laid into her, and he'd seen it again today—with Meg.

It was a fifteen minute drive to the palace, but Luca did it in eight—his silver car rattling around the tight bends at breakneck speed. Instead of turning off into the guarded private road to the palace, he carried on to the prison, not even taking the keys out of the ignition before he strode in.

'Where is she?'

The guard jumped to his feet, recognising Luca instantly and fumbling to cover his sordid trail—stubbing out a cigarette and ramming a bottle into a drawer.

'In the cell.' He gave a low laugh, which revealed black, rotting teeth. 'She says she wants a lawyer. I told her all the lawyers in Niroli are retained by you!'

'What else has she said?'

'She's crazy.' He tapped the side of his head a couple of times. 'She refuses her meals, refuses to sleep, or to put on the clothes we give her. She went crazy in there before—like an animal, pulling off the mattress, kicking at the walls, throwing her meal when we gave it to her. Now she says she is sister to Prince Alessandro….'

'What?' Luca barked. 'What exactly did she say?'

'That she came to the island to meet her brother—she gave his other name—the one he had before….'

'Alex Hunter?' Luca frowned, his mind racing. Was that what had happened—had the attraction that had flared the second he'd laid eyes on her actually been recognition?

Alessandro was his cousin—they shared the same grandfather, so if somehow he had a sister…?

'I want to talk to her.' It wasn't a request, it was an order, Luca's urgent words delivered almost in anger, and the guard knew better than to question it—just a slight raise of untidy eyebrows as he shrugged and led Luca to the cells.

She was adopted! As he followed the guard down the dank stairwell he replayed their earlier conversation over, recalling the details, and relief flooded him as he remembered what Meg had said. Even if she *were* somehow related to Alessandro, then it wasn't by blood—but it was a royal prince's sister who was locked up in a cell and about to be charged with theft—a scandal the family could do without just now.

For the old king's sake—for the honour of the family—the fact Alessandro's sister had been arrested for the attempted theft of the Niroli jewels, no less, was something that had to be kept quiet.

'*Aspetta*—wait!' Despite Luca's haste to get to her, there was one unsavoury duty that needed to be performed first—one last court with disaster before the king made his decision. Pulling out his wallet, Luca delivered his orders to the guard, hoping to God as he did so that the half-drunk bottle of whisky he had seen him shove into the drawer would be empty by the morning—that this blurry exchange would be nothing but a distant memory by dawn.

The cells were mainly empty apart from a couple of drunks sleeping it off, but the pubs and clubs hadn't closed yet. Luca knew that by morning the place would be rank with Niroli's low life. As he entered the dreary area that housed Meg, Luca knew that it wasn't duty that was driving him—as he made his way in, his eyes taking a moment to accustom to the dim lights, Luca knew it was her he was truly there for.

She was sitting on the simple metal bed, back rigid, staring fixedly ahead, not even turning as they approached, and Luca knew, quite simply, that she didn't belong in such a rank place.

Whatever emotions he'd been feeling before were paltry compared to what he felt now. He'd thought her beautiful, but realised it was a shallow description. Here, with her hair dark from sweat, her face a mess of dried blood and grime, and her top torn, sitting on the bare metal frame of the bed with a rudimentary attempt of a meal upturned on the floor beside her, he witnessed something in Meg far deeper and longer lasting than beauty. Despite the chaos of the room there was an elegance to her that seemed to reach somewhere deep inside him and twist his stomach, something about her that tugged at him. He'd always liked women, always enjoyed their company, but this ran deeper. This feeling Meg stirred wasn't about him, but instead about her and what he could do *for* her—only she mustn't know.

This isn't your doing!

There was an attempt at reason, to remind himself that it was her actions that had put her in this place—but it was futile. Whatever her reasons, whatever had driven her to steal last night, he wanted to know them—wanted so much more from Meg than he wanted from most women.

He wanted to get to know her....

Good or bad—he wanted all of her.

'Alzarsi!' Meg's grasp of the Italian language might be less than basic, but as the guard entered her cell and pulled her to her feet there was little room for misunderstanding and Meg did as she was told: she stood up. But nothing more— refusing to turn her head, refusing to acknowledge Luca Fierezza as he stepped into the tiny cell.

She'd known he was here—had heard his deep, angry voice for the last few moments—but whatever his reason for coming, it was too little, too late. The last couples of hours had been a nightmare: no one spoke more than a few words of English and, combined with Meg's few words of Italian, the police and guards had seemed to take pleasure in the chaos it had created. Taunting her when she'd asked for a lawyer or for them to contact the embassy, laughing in her face when Meg had written down Alex's name for them and tried to explain that until recently her brother had worked at the hospital. Then, after a rough body search, she had been thrown in the tiny, damp cell—which for Meg was the worst part of all, the tiny cell, the isolation, so reminiscent of her younger years it was impossible not to compare, not to relive the virtual prison of her childhood, impossible for it not to provoke a reaction. The guard bringing her a meal, ordering her to eat, had, for Meg, been the final straw and now, exhausted from her outburst, amidst the chaos she'd created, she stood before Luca.

'Meg, are you okay?' It was such a relief to hear English, her determination not to look at him, not to talk to him, weakened a touch, but she held on—still, even at this eleventh hour, trusting that order would prevail, that a lawyer, an official, *someone* would come and sort out this chaos.

'Meg, talk to me,' Luca insisted. 'I can help you.'

Her top lip sneered in disgust and somehow Luca knew she wasn't going to accept his offer of help, that, even if she was the guilty one, somehow it was he, Luca, she mistrusted. *'Aqua,'* Luca snapped to the guard, thinking on his feet, trying somehow to get her to realise that he was on her side. He barked orders in Italian to the guard, demanding he get food and something to clean up Meg's face with. Only when they were alone did he approach Meg, but she recoiled as if he were poison and with supreme effort he halted, stifling the instinct to take her in his arms and soothe her. 'Meg...' He stared at the paltry room, took in the upturned meal on the floor and struggled to find what to say, how to reach her. 'You should eat something....'

'I'd rather starve than eat what they bring me.' Even if it was laced with venom, at least she was talking, Luca conceded.

'You could be here for some time—you should change out of these dirty clothes, get some sleep. You need to eat—'

'Why?' Angry, defensive eyes turned to him. 'Why should I wear their clothes or sleep or eat at their command when I have done nothing wrong? Anyway, what is it to you? What exactly are you here for, Luca?'

'As I said, I am here to help you.'

He thought she might spit at him—her face was so sour with contempt she was barely recognisable.

'More likely, you're here to make sure that your handi-work has been carried out properly. Well, as you can see, it has been. Is this what happens when you refuse to sleep with the prince of Niroli?'

'It has nothing to do with that!' The guard was back and, taking the bowl of water and cloths he'd brought with him, Luca dismissed him, leading her to the bed where she reluctantly sat, examining the small cut in her eyebrow. 'I will clean your face. It is dirty in this cell—the wound will get infected.'

'I'll clean it,' Meg snarled, but he didn't listen, just calmly dipped the fabric into the water and bathed her wounds as the first sting of tears since her arrest reached her eyes. His hand was so supremely gentle, so tender, she couldn't help but compare it to the treatment the guards had given earlier, and for a second it was just easier somehow to let him help, to close her eyes as gently he removed the dried blood and dirt before pulling out of his pocket a heavy silk handkerchief and telling her to press it to her face.

'You will need a stitch or two. Do you know if the guard has arranged a doctor?'

'I'm sure that he has it on his list of people to call for me.'

Her sarcasm wasn't wasted on Luca, his eyes shuttering closed for a moment and she hoped it was in guilt, guilt for what he had done to her, but in that second he changed, his demeanour shifting from tender to practical.

'You stole from me, Meg—I saw the evidence myself. I had no choice but to call the police. You are here because you are a thief. Now we have to work out what to do with you.'

'Do with me?' Meg gave an incredulous laugh. 'And what the hell do you mean that I stole from you?'

'I've seen the evidence, Meg.'

'How?' She balled her fists to her temples in an attempt to calm down, the whole thing getting more ludicrous by the moment. She'd realised the guards thought her a common thief, that much she understood, but hearing it from Luca, realising he thought that of her, was almost more than she could take. 'How could you have seen something when it didn't even happen?'

'The jewels that were found in your bag are the Niroli family jewels, so, yes, you stole from me. Why you would do such a thing I do not know. Whatever trouble you are in I will try to help, try to understand, but it is imperative—'

'Luca—I am not a thief,' Meg broke in. 'I have no idea what you're talking about. All I want is a lawyer, someone to ring the embassy so that this mess can be sorted. I've never stolen a single thing in my life.'

It was like rewinding his life—watching the woman he adored furiously denying what he had witnessed—only this time he wouldn't back down. He was a man now—not a confused child. He was a royal prince and he would not be lied to, would not just *choose* to believe her because it was easier to.

'Don't lie to me!' His words were a roar, his six-foot-two frame jumping from the bed and towering over her. She was so convincing, so utterly, utterly convincing that if he hadn't seen the evidence himself, he'd have believed her—wanted to believe her—wanted to be taken in by this vixen's lies.

'I will not be lied to,' Luca repeated, but more calmly this time, speaking to her now as he would any of his staff that had overstepped the mark and needed to be pulled swiftly back into line. 'I am here to try to help you, but how can I do that when still you lie to me? I saw it with my own eyes, Meg. I saw you taking the jewels from the display—they were found in your backpack, wrapped in the top you were wearing last night.' On and on he went, each word damning her, each word confusing her further, because he clearly believed them, and all Meg knew was that it was imperative that Luca believe in her.

'I don't know what you saw or what you've been told, but

you're mistaken.' She stared right at him as she spoke. 'If you can't or won't believe me, then can you please just call a lawyer or the embassy for me in the morning?'

'It's Saturday tomorrow,' Luca pointed out, 'and it is a long weekend for the Feast—there can be no officials contacted till Tuesday, perhaps even Wednesday.'

'Then can you please try and get hold of my brother for me…?' Meg gulped back tears, her voice wobbling with fear as she realised that this nightmare wasn't anywhere near over and, though she was loath to ask Luca for any assistance, it was infinitely preferable to staying here. 'His name's Alex Hunter. He was working at the hospital—'

'Alessandro Fierezza is on his honeymoon,' Luca interrupted, 'on his way back to Australia. Alessandro is not going to be able to help you now.'

'Alessandro?' Meg gave a bewildered shake of her head. 'I don't know any Alessandro. I'm asking you to find my brother—'

'My cousin,' Luca brutally cut in, taking no pleasure as her proud face literally crumpled before his eyes, but his face remained impassive. He knew she needed him to be strong, that this fiery, independent woman wouldn't take a grain of his sympathy. 'Your brother is my cousin—get it? Alessandro is a royal prince—'

'No!' It didn't make sense, nothing today made any sense. Alex was a doctor, her brother, the most honourable man she knew, if he'd had news this big he'd have told her himself, face to face….

He'd wanted to.

The truth, however unpalatable, was starting to sink in. Alex had said the news was *huge*; could this have been it? Like Meg, Alex had been adopted, only at a much younger age, so his past was vague, but he was of Italian descent and the receptionist at the hospital had used the same name Luca was using now—Alessandro Fierezza…

Burying her face in her hands, Meg struggled for control, tried to glimpse some way out of this hellish mess. Drunken, loud voices were coming from upstairs, the tiny cells starting to fill with undesirables, and she was trapped here till God knew when….

'I can sort this mess out for you, Meg.'

'How?' Peeling down her fingers, Meg stared up at him.

'I just can….' Luca's Adam's apple bobbed as he swallowed hard, unsure how Meg would react to what he had done, but somehow guessing she wouldn't take it particularly well. 'I can make this go away.'

'You mean you'll bribe someone!' Appalled, Meg shook her head, but Luca was insistent.

'You are the sister of a prince—therefore you do not belong here. The family cannot afford the scandal at this time.'

'The only scandal is that I've been locked up and accused of a crime I didn't commit,' Meg retorted. 'I don't need you covering my tracks, Luca. It's your family that will suffer if I stay here.'

'It will cause shame for your brother,' Luca pointed out. But Meg wasn't about to be subdued.

'Then you clearly don't know Alex,' she flared back. 'He'd tell me to fight my case. Unlike you, Alex would believe a woman who was speaking the truth.'

'Then your brother is a fool,' Luca retorted. 'We both know you lie, we both know the truth. You can stay here and rot, then. I have offered assistance. I have done the right thing by Alessandro. It is not my fault if you will not accept it!'

This was getting nowhere; Luca had quickly realised that. He could hear the processing of the new prisoners taking place upstairs, knew that at any given moment he might be recognised. If Meg didn't come with him now, he would have to leave her here to fight her case alone.

Staring down at her, defiant, wary and so very, very scared, Luca knew what he had to do, knew that she was too proud for charity, too proud to back down—so he did what he did best.

Cut her a deal—Luca style.

Let her think she had a choice, let her think she had a chance of winning.

'Maybe there is another way,' Luca mused out loud. 'Last night I said I wanted to spend time with you; last night I explained I wanted the pleasure of your company….'

'You had that today,' Meg attempted, but Luca shook his head.

'Forget today, Meg. Now I know how low you stoop, the offer drops. I will not bribe the guard, but I *will* pay your bail—I will assure him that I am taking care of you and that you will return for your hearing with suitable representation.'

'And in return?' For the first time since he'd arrived Luca actually smiled. 'You mean you want me as your *puttana*,' Meg spat. It was one of the few Italian words she did know— she had heard it several times since she'd been locked up, and it was one of the few words that needed little translation. He was literally offering to buy her company. 'You're not doing this out of some false sense of duty to Alex, you're offering this because of how I look!'

'Well, you don't look very good at this moment,' Luca retorted, 'but I think you will scrub up very nicely. This is a good offer, Meg,' he continued. 'You can stay here and take your chances with the guards and your fellow prisoners, or

I will pay your bail and you can come with me and stay in luxurious surrounds until Tuesday, when I will arrange full access to one of the best lawyers on the mainland.'

'And for the privilege—I'll have to share your bed!'

'Of course.' He stared down at his watch, tapped an impatient foot as he awaited her decision, and her first instinct was to slap him, to spit on his arrogant face and tell him where the hell he could put his offer, but something held her back. Realisation sank in that she was here for the duration. Her passport had already been taken, her belongings locked away. Here she had no rights, no possessions, but as the prince's mistress she would be afforded decent legal representation—could get out of this mess through the correct channels instead of offering some sleazy bribe.

She still had a choice.

She would *choose* to eat at his table, *choose* to share his bed, but she wouldn't share her heart…. Luca Fierezza had enough money and power to buy her company for a short while, but he would never hold her heart.

CHAPTER EIGHT

THEY DROVE IN SILENCE to the palace, Luca's car hugging the beach road, the palace easily visible thanks to a vast moon hanging low in the sky, but despite the warm night air as she'd stepped from the prison to the custody of her new jailer, Meg had started violently shivering, so she sat now huddled in the passenger seat wearing Luca's jacket.

'Why aren't we going to the casino?'

'You will be recognised at the casino—you are on the black list. Until we can arrange for some new clothes, your hair to be done differently, you will have to stay away from there.'

'But surely…'

'The staff at the palace are discreet—that is why I am taking you there.'

'Won't they at least want to know who I am?'

'Why would they?' Luca shrugged and she glanced over at him, taking in his perfect profile, the sheer maleness he radiated, the absolute arrogant beauty of him, and the unpalatable truth was further affirmed. They wouldn't ask questions because this was clearly a regular occurrence—oh, not the rescue from the jail, but clearly the palace staff were more than used to Luca arriving home at all hours with a woman in tow! 'I will arrange a doctor to come and tend to your cut.'

'I don't need a doctor, and anyway,' Meg added, 'surely *he* would ask questions.'

'Why would he? I pay for his discretion,' Luca responded with all the arrogance of the truly rich, but he did at least concede that her arrival might cause some issues, because as the gates to a private road slid open and the car approached he momentarily stopped and, with the engine idling, he turned to face her.

'This is what we do. I tell my family the truth—you are Alessandro's sister, you came to the island to look him up not realising he had already left. That is why I am taking care of you.'

'So am I here as Alex's sister or your mistress?' Meg quipped, but Luca, as always, had an answer.

'Both.' He turned and gave her a dry smile. 'Just remember, though, your first duty is to me.'

'And the cut?' Meg snapped. 'Did that come in the line of duty?'

'Jet-skiing.' Luca gave a rare smile—clearly happy with his fabrication. 'You had an accident jet-skiing today when you were exploring. You were hoping your brother would be able to patch you up.'

'That's not the truth,' Meg pointed out.

'Oh, but from now on it is.' Black eyes bore into hers. 'You really don't expect me to tell them you were attempting to steal the Niroli jewels, do you?'

'No, because that isn't the truth, either.'

He didn't respond, just pulled off the handbrake and drove along the stretch of road towards the palace, orange groves flanking their progress. Despite the vile day, despite an exhausted mind that just wanted to switch from all that was happening, Meg couldn't help but be impressed at the sheer splendour of the building she'd till now only glimpsed from a distance. A huge fourteenth-century castle, it stood proud on the edge of the ocean as if carved out of the rocks itself, and Meg could scarcely believe that this was where she would be calling home for the next few days.

Even before the car had slid to a halt, despite the lateness of the hour the door was opened by waiting staff, but Luca barely greeted them, just exchanging a few words with a burly, suited gentleman before taking a stunned and shivering Meg by the arm and leading her to a side entrance, which Meg soon realised was the access to the palace's private apartments.

'That was my bodyguard, Luigi,' Luca needlessly explained his earlier conversation. 'He is annoyed that again I did not tell him I was leaving the casino. I will speak with him in the morning—if you need to leave the palace for any reason, he is to drive and accompany you.'

'I don't need an escort,' Meg responded tightly.

'Perhaps not,' Luca answered as he pushed open the door to his apartment, 'but since I signed your bail papers you are my responsibility. I want to be sure I know where you are—and, more importantly, that you will return.'

She was too tired to be indignant or even attempt a smart retort. She stepped inside Luca's luxurious apartment. Someone on the gate must have alerted the staff, because even though it was only a matter of minutes since the car had entered the palace grounds there was a fire taking hold in the magnificent marble fireplace and the lights were all on. A large whisky had been poured and set on an occasional table, which Luca downed in one gulp while Meg still stood at the doorway taking in her surrounds. Lavishly furnished, the apartment had been exquisitely refurbished—somehow managing to combine the fourteenth-century décor with *all* the luxuries of the twenty-first century. Vast high walls were broken by voile curtains that swept the shuttered windows, a papal purple carpet runner softened the cool Italian marble floor. The apartment was a virtual treasure trove of antiques and under any other circumstances Meg would have been thrilled to explore, but all she could do was stand and shiver, overwhelmed with fatigue, and Luca, for the first time since the prison, was gently perceptive, guiding her limp body across to the warmth of the fire.

'Even in summer the castle is cool at night,' Luca explained, but there was a worried edge to his voice, his hand running over her forehead as if she were a child and he were checking her temperature, 'The doctor will be here soon.'

'You've called him?' Meg frowned, worried that she couldn't remember, but Luca shook his head. 'I told Luigi to take care of it.'

There was clearly no trouble arranging a rapid house call when you were Niroli royalty, and the doctor arrived shortly afterwards. Any worries Meg might have had about explaining her injuries were quashed when Luca did what little talking was required.

'You need two stitches on your…' Luca tapped his own eyebrow by explanation, then gave a small wince as the doctor said something else to him. 'He says he can give you an injection to make it numb before he stitches you, but that will hurt as much as if he just goes ahead and puts in the stitches without it.'

'No injections!'

'*Il donatore il suo anestetico locale.*' Luca fired at the doctor in rapid Italian. Too quick for Meg to grasp.

'What did you say?' Meg asked as the doctor nodded.

'I said that he was to numb it first for you.'

'Well, that's not what I want. Can you please tell him to just go ahead and do the stitches?' Meg countered.

'But it will hurt.'

'So will the anaesthetic,' Meg pointed out, 'and next time you decide to act as a translator for me, please, allow me to answer for myself!' As Luca opened his mouth to argue, Meg got there first. 'What is he saying now?'

'That he will use the finest silk, and that with make-up the cut will not show. After he has tended your wound you are to bathe and sleep…' He checked his understanding of the order of events with the doctor, who was setting up his tools, then elaborated. 'You are to bathe, have a light supper and then sleep—he will come and check on you again some time over the weekend. I'll have the house-keeper run you a bath.'

'I'd prefer a shower.' Meg screwed her eyes closed as the doctor poured out antiseptic and proceeded to clean her wound.

'Would you?' Luca snapped. 'Or are you just determined to contradict everything I say?'

'Yes to both,' Meg answered cheekily. As Luca let out a hiss of indignation, she caught his eyes and gave him a tiny glimmer of a smile, which, after a beat of hesitation, he reluctantly reciprocated. 'Let's just get this over with.'

The stitches hurt, though not that much, and Meg bit hard on her lip as the needle went in and out. When Luca reached for her hand to comfort her, she pulled it back, preferring to see this through by herself.

'You are very brave,' Luca commented once the doctor had gone and finally they were alone. 'Not many people would sit there so still. In fact…' His voice trailed off—the only other person he could think of who would react as Meg had, who would barely offer a reaction as their wounds were tended, was his mother.

'Can I have my shower now please?' Supremely polite, she evaded comment on his observations.

'Of course.' Luca nodded, attempting normal, trying to blot out the pictures that were forming in his mind, to stifle the wells of emotion she produced in him without even trying.

What had happened to her?

The question buzzed in his mind as he led her to the bathroom. There was no need to check that she had everything she needed when she was in the Niroli palace—the sparkling bathroom had every luxury required for an unexpected female guest—Luca's thick, white fluffy towels were warming on the heated rails, new toothbrush still in its wrapper, expensive moisturisers and rich, handmade soaps. But her weariness troubled him and Luca, for the first time ever, turned on the taps for a shower he wasn't invited to partake in.

'Call if you need anything,' Luca offered, though he knew that she wouldn't.

Who *had* hurt her?

Heading into the lounge room, he stood as the supper tray was delivered and the maid poured him another shot of whisky. He raised the glass to his lips once she stepped outside, but instead of drinking it, instead of taking refuge in the sharp, sedating liquid, with a curse, a howl of pain almost, he hurled the glass into the fireplace, watching the heavy crystal crack and splinter, not even blinking at the flare of blue light as the alcohol momentarily ignited.

What was it with this Meg woman?

This thief who had crept into his heart—what was it with

her that moved him so, unleashed something within him, forced him to examine the murky waters of his own life? She was like a drug—like the most dangerous of drugs, one taste and he had been reeled in, hooked by an internal craving for something he couldn't define, something that could surely only end in grief if it was sustained. And like any addiction it was mired in secrets. There was no hearing on Tuesday—the guard had been easily paid off, Meg's belongings put in the back of the car—but if she knew that, she'd be gone in an instant. She was only here because he'd supposedly paid for her, the woman he was starting to know was way too proud to accept a sympathy vote....

He must treat her as he would any mistress—demand of her what he did of all his women: engaging company, immaculate presentation and a healthy dose of sex to boot— then get her off the island, purge her from his mind once the festivities were over.... Clenching his fists beside him, Luca blanched at that prospect of losing her, whilst simultaneously baulking at the prospect of keeping her.

She was trouble.

No, Luca corrected, with sadness—she was troubled.

'Are you okay?'

Strange that it was Meg asking him the question, that someone so fragile, in such dire straits, was asking someone so seemingly strong. But there she was standing with her hair dripping, wrapped in a huge bathrobe, her fingers pulling the wrap of the neckline tighter; vulnerable, nervous and, Luca realised, utterly, utterly adorable.

'I'm fine.' Luca nodded. 'There is hot chocolate and sweet breads... I don't know what you would call it,' he attempted, expecting her to refuse, quietly pleased when she tentatively sat down, taking a sip of the warm sweet drink before parting the pastry with long, delicate fingers, then hesitating.

'Come on, eat,' Luca prompted, frowning as her body stiffened and she dropped the pastry down onto the plate.

'I'm not hungry.'

'You didn't eat in the prison,' Luca pointed out. 'You remember the doctor said that you should have some supper.'

'So?' Meg shrugged. 'It was a suggestion, not a prescription.'

'Suit yourself.' Luca gave a tight shrug, but he was getting rattled now; he had rescued her, brought her here to his apartment, arranged a doctor, in fact he had done more for this woman in the few hours he had known her than he *ever* had for anyone before. Yet, far from being grateful, she had the audacity to speak back at him. In fact, Luca realised, he was no closer to her now than he had been back in the Niroli kitchen. Again she was keeping him at arm's length, treating him with mild disdain as if *he* somehow wasn't good enough for *her*. 'Is there anyone you would like to ring?'

'I don't fancy my chances of getting a lawyer from the embassy at this hour of the night.'

'They will tell you exactly what I have—until your case is heard you are not entitled to your passport. What about your parents?' He was holding out the phone to her, offering her a link to the outside world, his hand completely steady as Meg's reached out for the phone, but if Meg had looked up she'd have seen his nervous swallow. 'I mean your adopted parents....'

'*They* are my parents,' Meg corrected hotly, but the fire in her died a bit as, after a brief hesitation, she pulled back the hand that had reached out, curled up tighter on the chair and started to comb her damp hair. 'I don't want to worry them.'

'That is surely their job—to worry!'

'As you said—there's nothing anyone can do. Calling my parents isn't going to make a scrap of difference. Once I've spoken to a lawyer, once I know what's happening, *then* I'll let them know.'

Never had she wanted her parents more. The thought of ringing them, hearing their reassuring voices amidst this blizzard of confusion, to ask for their guidance, their assistance, was a temptation that was almost impossible to resist—but she couldn't do it to them…again.

Combing her hair furiously, Meg recalled how they'd worried about her travelling. It had taken weeks, no, months to reassure them, to tell them she was ready for this, to assure them she'd be okay. Meg closed her eyes, imagining the ringing of the phone piercing their afternoon—they were probably out on the decking, enjoying the last of the sunshine before evening descended. The thought of spinning them into anxiety, of *again* being the source of their pain, was the only reason Meg refused Luca's offer.

'You look a lot better,' Luca observed as she finished combing her hair.

'I feel it,' Meg admitted, making the stilted conversation just a little easier. 'I was already desperate for a shower by the time I got to the casino, covered in suntan oil and sand. It seems like ages ago….'

'A lot has happened since then.'

'I still can't believe it about Alex.' Meg gave a bewildered laugh. 'Though I actually *do* believe it.'

'You are adopted also,' Luca said. 'Who knows? Maybe you are royalty, too—isn't that every adopted child's dream?'

'Not mine.' Meg took a nervous sip of her drink. 'In fact, I spent most of my childhood *hoping* to find out I was adopted.' When Luca gave her a curious look, Meg reluctantly elaborated. 'I was adopted when I was much older than Alex.'

'How old?'

Meg gave a tight shrug. 'When I was twelve.'

'What happened to your parents?' Luca's voice was curious rather than sympathetic. 'Were they killed? Did they—?'

'My *biological* parents are alive and well—physically anyway.'

'I don't understand.' Luca frowned, treading carefully now, hearing the emphasis on the word biological and realising there was considerable pain behind the tight, rigid expression Meg was wearing. 'When you say physically...'

'Some people should never have children,' Meg said firmly, then pushed the conversation firmly back to its original direction. 'You say that Alex is married?'

'Very happily,' Luca replied, 'and very quickly! She's a nurse, her name is Amelia.'

Which ended that conversation. The tension was increasing as she put down her empty cup, her drink finished, her wounds tended, the doctor's orders loosely followed all bar one....

'It is time for bed,' Luca said, stating the inevitable.

'Okay.' Her voice was small, a flash of nervousness darting in those gorgeous blue eyes as she stood up and, though Luca had never wanted her more, wanted so much to take her in his arms and kiss away all the horrors of the day, he also knew that wasn't what she really needed and, for the first time in his spoiled life, Luca pushed his own needs aside.

'I will sleep on the couch.' Luca broke the interminable silence. 'The doctor said you needed to rest.'

'I thought...' Meg gave a nervous, embarrassed swallow,

incredibly grateful for the reprieve, but confused all the same. 'I thought that I was supposed to be—'

'My mistress?' Luca finished the difficult sentence for her, his voice suddenly harsh. 'I don't think somehow you fit the bill tonight—did you not think to look in the mirror when you left the bathroom?'

She was too damned exhausted to be cross, too damned grateful not to have to be involved in some extended sexual marathon to answer back. The bed was soft as she climbed in, the heavy Italian linen cool on her aching limbs, her exhausted body stretching out gratefully, but still she couldn't relax, the whole day just too bizarre, too overwhelming to switch off just because she closed her eyes. She tried, tried not to think about all that had happened, her mind buzzing like a chainsaw till finally a fitful sleep descended, only there was no solace there—back in a prison cell, only the walls were different; pretty, pale-pink walls, the grimy, grey prison blanket replaced now by a soft, pink one, toys smiling down at her from the wall.

Back in the bedroom of her childhood—seemingly perfect; sinister in its deception.

But unlike then, this time when she cried out in her sleep it didn't go unheeded; this time, when she called out in terror, someone answered….

For Luca it wasn't an effort to hold her and not intimately touch her. Meg could never have known the supreme effort it had taken him to be so cruel to her before she'd gone to bed. Holding her in his arms now, shushing her back to a sweeter sleep, for the first time he was in bed with a woman and it wasn't sex that was on his mind, but the woman herself.

Tonight he would hold her, Luca decided, breaking his

promise, slipping dangerously off the wagon as he pulled the sheets around her slender shoulders, breathed in the sweet scent of her damp hair; tonight he would allow himself the luxury of looking after her…then, tomorrow, it was back to business.

CHAPTER NINE

'BREAKFAST IS HERE!'

A sharp rap at the door and Luca's even sharper voice had Meg waking with a start and the mother of all mortification.

If she'd made wild passionate love to him she'd have felt better—but waking up in the empty bed, gradually orientating herself, piecing together the previous days, Meg cringed with embarrassment. Not at being labelled a thief or finding herself locked up, nor at the shame of being arrested in front of a crowd of curious onlookers, but at what had taken place long after the day was over: crying out in her sleep— reaching out to Luca when he'd come, holding onto him throughout the night....

Letting out a low moan, Meg rolled over, inhaling his heavy, unmistakable scent that lingered on the sheets, seeing the indent in the pillow, the bed still warm from where he'd lain beside her—wondering how she could summon the nerve to head out to the lounge and face him....

'Good morning!' Wearing a false smile brighter than the sun blazing through the windows, Meg breezed into the living room, curiously deflated that her grand entrance was masked by the vast broadsheet he was engrossed in as he sat at a beautifully decorated table. The heady scent of fresh flowers that hadn't been there last night mingled with the aroma of coffee. There were crisp white napkins and heavy silver cutlery fit for a five-star restaurant—a world away from the backpacker hostels that had been home for the last few months.

'*Buongiorno.*' He flicked a hand in the vague direction of a vast silver trolley that had been wheeled into the room. 'Help yourself to breakfast.'

It wasn't just the table that was elaborate—clearly room service took on a whole new meaning when you were living at the palace. Meg would have quickly helped herself had there been anything as straightforward as cereal, but the trolley groaned under the weight of various hams, sickly pastries and an array of olives and syrupy fruits. What was it with the Italians that their breakfasts looked more like an evening meal? Meg had loved France with the crusty rolls and hot chocolate breakfasts, but this was all way too much.

'If you would prefer a cooked breakfast I can call the chef.'

'No, no.' Meg shook her head, her stomach curdling at the thought. Even though she was well into her recovery, Meg was still nervous of eating in front of strangers, especially at this hour of the morning—so, bypassing the meats and oil-soaked delicacies, she fashioned something similar to the breakfast she had enjoyed in France, taking a thick slice of olive bread smothered in rock salt and adding a dash of coffee as thick as treacle to a glass of warm milk poured from a heavy silver jug.

'Come!' Impatiently Luca gestured for her to join him. 'I have to go into work shortly—is that all you are having?' He frowned. 'It's no trouble to call the chef....'

'I'm fine—thank you.'

'Tonight we eat out,' Luca said. 'Away from here, away

from the casino—there is a nice bayside restaurant I will take you to. There they do the best rainbow mullet you will ever taste. It is the island's speciality dish….' He frowned at her lack of enthusiasm. 'Is there a problem?'

'Of course not.'

'Only you do not seem particularly talkative.'

'It's seven in the morning,' Meg pointed out. He might be paying for her company, but surely he didn't expect an all-singing, all-dancing production at this hour. 'I'm never particularly talkative this early.'

But, clearly, he did.

'Well, I'm sorry to have woken you!' Luca's sarcasm was biting. 'Perhaps tomorrow you can ensure it's the other way around.'

Clearly, Luca liked his women bright and breezy and ready to entertain at all hours. Picking up his newspaper, less than amused, Luca didn't look up as he spoke. 'I will arrange for a stylist to come over this morning—do you have any preferences?'

'Preferences?' Because he wasn't watching now, Meg dipped her bread into her coffee. 'I can go out and get some clothes this morning.'

'Dressed in your robe?' Luca peered over his paper. 'Or rather, in my robe? And tell me—how do you intend to pay for your purchases? You could always cash your cheque, I guess, or sell a few jewels. Oh, sorry, I forgot—all your belongings have been impounded!' With a dry smile he returned to the business page. 'Oh, and I'll send someone from the hair salon too,' he added as an afterthought. 'Your hair really does need attending to—it is very brassy.'

Where, Meg wondered, had the tender man who had held her, comforted her last night disappeared to? But then again she was almost relieved to see the back of him. This version of Luca she could deal with—life was so much easier when she could hate him!

'Anything else?' Meg checked, bristling at the insult—brassy it might be, but that was from swimming in the ocean and hours in the blistering sun. She'd never dyed her hair in her life. 'Is there anything else you'd like me to fix so I look the part for you?'

'That is women's business.' Luca shrugged. 'You can surprise me—speak with the beautician. She can do the wax or whatever you need—I do not need to know such things.'

'What about a lawyer?' Meg watched as his knuckles tightened around the newspaper, practically curling it into a ball as she spoke on. 'While you're on the phone arranging my minimakeover, could you find the time to arrange the lawyer we'd agreed to?'

'Public holiday.' Luca shrugged.

'You know—' Meg put down her mug '—your English is incredibly bad when you want it to be.'

'And your manners are appalling when you think no one is watching.' Luca finally deigned to put down his newspaper, catching her red-handed as she dunked her bread once again. 'And when you date royalty, someone always is—it would serve you well to remember that.

'Right, I will put all the arrangements in place and my mother will come with you to the day spa.'

'Your mother?' Meg gave an incredulous grin. 'It's a bit early to be meeting the in-laws, isn't it?'

'Don't be facetious!' Luca reproached. 'You are Alessandro's sister, of course I would introduce you to her. Anyway, tomorrow the formal celebration for the Feast of Niroli takes place. There will be a ball here in the palace. I expect you to attend. My mother will tell you how to behave. She knows how a lady should act—it would be useful for you to listen.'

'I thought you wanted to keep things quiet,' Meg attempted. 'What if someone recognises me?'

'Believe me, Meg—' Luca gave a tight smile '—once you are groomed and more suitably dressed…no one will recognise you. I can also assure you my mistresses do not spend their time *sitting* around to fill the hours.'

'Of course not,' Meg challenged. 'They're too busy preening themselves and voiding themselves of any opinions in preparation for the master's return!' She'd gone too far—at least further than Prince Luca's women usually did, because his swarthy skin was pale as he turned to face her, his eyes black as coal as he silenced her with a look.

'I make no apology for liking beautiful women, Meg.' His eyes narrowed as he walked towards her, his fingers reaching out and cupping her chin, assessing her, appraising her, as if he were purchasing some sort of show pony. 'You know, for someone so very pretty you spoil it with your bitterness, your—' With his free hand he snapped his fingers, summoning a word that wouldn't come, and settling for one that hurt way more. 'You *infect* yourself with your anger, your animosity.

'Remember—if it wasn't for me, you would be rotting in jail for the next week or two.'

'I've survived worse,' Meg retorted, defiant perhaps, yet speaking the truth, but Luca shook his head.

'You were scared when I came and rescued you—and the night hadn't even started. You want to go back, then I will take you there now—just say the word.'

He would, Meg knew that, and she also knew that if jail had been hell before it would be worse on her return. She could almost feel the rough, greedy hands of the guard on her and her eyes widened in terror, her brow beading with sweat. Luca must have seen it, because somehow he changed, the anger replaced by confusion.

'Here you have everything—the best of everything—and still you fight me,' he said.

'I won't… I'm not.' Her breath was coming out fast and rapid, the thought of returning to the cell filling her with horror. At least here she had relative freedom, and there was a chance she would get a decent lawyer, but, more to the point, here she knew she would be looked after, that somehow Luca Fierezza, with all his pompous arrogance, would take care of her. 'I'm not fighting you, Luca. I'm looking forward to getting dressed up. I'm looking forward to the Feast.' And she expected a gleam of triumph in those angry black eyes, but he blinked in confusion at the change in her, the hand gripping her face loosening. 'I won't let you down.'

Within an hour of Luca leaving, as promised, there was a knock on the door and a middle-aged woman entered, her greeting brief but effusive, kissing Meg on both cheeks and introducing herself as Laura.

'Luca's mother?'

'That is right.' Her English wasn't as good as Luca's, but she explained she was here to help her with her choices. Just as Meg was about to ask what she meant, the question was answered by the arrival of not a dresser with a couple of samples wrapped in a carry suit, but endless racks being wheeled into the apartment, and not just dresses either— underwear, bathing suits, shoes, nightdresses.

'My son, he thinks of everything,' Laura said proudly as

Meg rather timidly approached the clothes. 'Come, Meg,' Laura said impatiently. 'We set to work!'

That was the understatement of the millennium. Clearly any mistress of Luca's, however temporary, was expected to look the part—and once her closet was filled with the smartest Italian fashion pieces and Meg was rather more suitably dressed, a car was summoned and Meg was being whisked to the day spa at breakneck speed, only the lights and sirens missing, in an effort to repair her 'brassy' hair.

'Don't worry.' With Meg placed in front of a mirror, a hairdresser tutting as she examined Meg's split ends, Laura gave a sympathetic smile and delivered the most stunning backhander. 'She is a miracle worker, I tell you. She can fix anything!'

Clearly used to being thoroughly spoiled, Laura had a facial as Meg's hair was 'dealt with', and at first they chatted amicably. Thankfully Laura didn't ask too many questions about Alex or her arrival in Niroli, just gave Meg a few tips on dealing with her new status as the sister of Niroli royalty.

'Luca will look after everything—the best thing you can say if the press ask a question is nothing.'

'I'm sure no one's really that interested in what I have to say,' Meg answered as Laura gave her a questioning frown.

'Come—you are surely not that naïve. Any woman on my son's arm generates interest, especially now he might become King.'

'Luca?' The hairdresser stepped back as Meg's head spun around.

'The king's health is failing,' Laura responded. 'Why not Luca? Your brother, he chooses his career over his country—

so now the attention turns to my son—' knowing eyes held Meg's '—and, of course, his beautiful bride-to-be."

'I'm not Luca's bride-to-be.' Meg jumped as if she'd been branded. 'We've only just met—it's hardly—'

'I tease you.' Laura smiled but it didn't quite reach her eyes. 'Still, that is what the press will say. When Luca is seen with anyone there is always speculation, but especially now. That is why it is imperative you behave properly. After we are finished here we have lunch back at the palace—I tell you then how you should behave with Luca.'

There was little chance of anyone at the casino recognising her, because back at the apartment, staring into the magnificent antique mirror over the fireplace, Meg barely recognised herself.

Her sun-bleached hair was but a memory now. Superbly toned down to a soft caramel-blond, it fell in a thick, straight, glossy curtain. Her complexion was smooth, her cheekbones impossibly visible thanks to the skill of the make-up artist—and she truly was an artist. With each stroke of her brush, with each dab of her finger she had sculpted Meg's face till it was almost unrecognisable—her blue eyes huge now, her already full lips glossy and pouting like a fashion model on the cover of a magazine. Even her body seemed to have changed. The dresser had crowed in delight at Meg's tall, svelte figure, but now as she stood and stared in the mirror, as perfect as the image supposedly was, Meg couldn't help but feel disappointed. The soft curves she'd fought so hard for had been all but eradicated in the simple, elegant shift dress, her legs impossibly long and slender in the highest of sandals.

'Pour his drink.' Laura's words echoed in her head as Meg followed protocol. 'Welcome him home with a smile.'

* * *

What the hell had he done?

Walking into the lounge, for once Luca was lost for words. Oh, he was used to beautiful women, perfect make-up, perfect hair. That was what he liked—that was what he insisted on, after all; but watching Meg walk over, holding out his drink to him, a smile forced on her made-up mouth, softly enquiring about his day, it was almost grief that hit him. Where was the feisty, independent lady he had left here this morning? Where was the tender, fragile woman he had held in his arms last night?

'How was work?'

'Long.' Luca flashed an on-off smile. 'How did you get on today?'

'Great, the day spa was wonderful…'

'And my mother?'

'Charming.' Meg's smile was as stilted as his, but then she relented a touch, offering an observation, even if it wasn't expected from her.

'She was lovely, actually—she clearly adores you.'

'She can be a bit overbearing, but she means well.'

'I like her,' Meg mused, 'or I think I would if…' Her voice trailed off as she remembered her place—remembered there would be no getting to know anyone. Neither time nor protocol allowed. 'What time is the restaurant booked for?' Meg forced an even bigger smile. 'I'm really looking forward to dinner.'

'Dinner,' he said stoutly, 'will be served when I choose to arrive.'

'Perfect.' Meg's smile barely moved.

Whistling through his teeth, Luca picked up the telephone and ordered his bodyguard to meet with them, wondering again what the hell he had done.

* * *

'Just smile,' Luca said taking her arm as they approached the restaurant. 'If anyone tries to stop and talk just smile graciously and keep moving.'

'Of course.' Nervous and trying not to show it, Meg took in a deep breath as the restaurant doors opened, hearing the gasp of delight from the clientele as their hefty dinner bill was more than justified—a night dining in the same restaurant as Luca Fierezza giving all present a tale to be regaled later.

'The food here is superb.' Luca chatted on as if it were just the two of them, clearly used to waiters flitting around and his bodyguards seated at the next table, clearly not minding a jot that the whole restaurant was watching—but for Meg it was a living hell, each morsel of deliciously prepared food like a dry rock in her throat, each attempt at meaningless conversation drying up by the second sentence.

'Really superb,' Meg agreed, cutting up the damned rainbow mullet and rueing the fact it was an Italian prince she was with—they were only starting the main meal and were already four courses in!

They'd started with antipasto, but like no other Meg had experienced. Each mouthful had been a taste sensation; in fact, Meg had never tasted an olive that tasted so much like an olive—though she hadn't attempted to explain that to Luca, just demurely murmured her approval when the plate was removed. Then had come shrimp salad, which Meg had actually enjoyed, the salad drizzled in Niroli Virgin Olive and Orange Oil—a local delicacy, Luca had told her, and she could see why. If Australian customs had allowed, Meg would have been sorely tempted to blow her budget and ship a lifetime supply home.

For Meg, though, the real hard work started when the pasta arrived.

Three huge squares of ravioli, each packed with gourmet fillings and drizzled with thick cheese sauce.

'These are my favourite.' Luca smiled as he poised his knife and fork. '*Salute!*'

'*Salute.*' Meg beamed, taking a hefty slug of water and bravely soldiering on.

'Is there a problem, Meg?' Watching her push her food around the plate, Luca frowned.

'None at all,' Meg said brightly. 'It's delicious. So, how was your—?'

'Four times tonight you have asked about my day,' Luca broke in, 'and three times you have said my mother is charming. We have discussed the weather, the food, even the rate of exchange—'

'I'm sorry you find my company boring.' Meg flashed her eyes at him.

'I didn't say that.' Luca's voice was irritated. 'I just—'

'Just what, Luca?' Putting down her knife and fork with a clatter, Meg struggled to keep her voice down, the strain catching up with her, the disappointment in his eyes as he looked over at her choking her. Yet no one, not even Luigi sitting a mere table away, could have guessed the conversation was anything but amicable, her rigid smile still in place as she told Luca exactly what she thought. 'You rudely tell me I don't look the part, you tell me I am too angry and hostile, you tell me I have appalling manners—so now, when I'm dressed appropriately, when I'm speaking dutifully and keeping my elbows well off the table, suddenly you're bored! Now, if you'll excuse me, I'm going to the bathroom.' Placing her napkin on the table, Meg excused herself, then changed her mind, her voice deathly quiet, but loud enough that Luca could hear, her smile still in place but her eyes saying otherwise. 'Just what is it that you want me to be? You keep changing the rules, Luca. I am doing what was asked of me—tonight I look the part, tonight I am good enough to share your bed and dine at your table—'

'And purge afterwards—' Gripping her wrist, he caught her as she turned to go, almost immediately realising he'd gone too far because the look of sheer horror on her face could never be manufactured, her voice hoarse with emotion when finally she found it.

'Can we leave now please?'

'I'm sorry.' They were being driven from the restaurant, Meg's face flaming beneath her foundation as they headed back to the palace. 'It was just an off-the-cuff comment—I was angry. I had no idea it would upset you so much.'

'You don't know me at all, Luca.'

She felt like asking to be let out, asking Luigi to stop so she could run, just take her chances and run as far away from everything as possible, claustrophobic at the prospect of returning to the vast palace with him, whilst conceding there was no space big enough to allow her to hide from Luca. It was as if he could see inside her, every word he uttered exposing more and more of her, peeling her away till there would surely be nothing left.

'We will walk the last part.' They were inside the palace grounds now and Luca helped her out of the car, speaking in Italian to his guards while Meg stood gulping in the cool night air, grateful when the car slipped away into the darkness. 'Always I have to tell people where I go.' His deep voice had a low growl to it. 'I am in my own home, yet still I have to give my route. I tell them we walk along the beach. Is that okay?'

She gave a silent nod.

'I hate having to account for every move—that is why I prefer normally to stay at the casino. Not that I will be able to if I become…' He didn't finish, and, according to the rules she'd been privy to today, Meg should have left it there, should have known better than to pry or prolong a conversation he wanted to terminate, but it was so much easier to talk about him than her now, so much easier to dwell on his problems than her own.

'Will you have to give up the casino, then, if you become King?'

For the longest time he didn't answer, just walked on in silence, till they came to a gorgeous stretch of beach, Luca waiting as Meg took off her sandals. 'You can leave them there,' Luca said when she picked them up to carry them. 'No one will take them; this is a private beach.'

'It's stunning,' Meg breathed. She'd seen plenty of beautiful beaches both at home and on her travels, but if there was a piece of paradise on earth then this surely was it—the most beautiful land reserved for the most beautiful people. White sand as soft as powder dusted beneath her bare feet, the castle a stunning backdrop, the sea warm as occasionally it lapped at her feet.

'And it could all be mine.' Instead of staring out to the ocean Luca stared back at the island, but there was no expectancy in his voice, just weariness…. 'I could rule it all.'

'Do you want to?'

'Would you?'

She thought long and hard before answering, the question so hypothetical it was almost impossible to imagine how she might feel in the circumstances. Only it wasn't hypothetical for Luca. She glanced over at his brooding face and tried to fathom for a moment his existence—one where every movement, every action was open to scrutiny, tried to fathom the price he paid for his lavish existence.

'I wouldn't want it,' Meg admitted finally. 'But then I'm such a private person, I just couldn't imagine being such…'

'Public property.' Luca chose the words for her. 'I was born into this, I have lived all my life in this goldfish bowl, yet it has taken till now for me to accept it. Now I have the casino, now I have a chance to be just Luca for a few hours, it is manageable—but if I become King then all that goes.'

'Does it have to?'

'There are rules—if you are a prince there are always rules.' Despite several thousand dollars of Italian silk suit, Luca lowered himself and stretched out on the sand, gesturing for Meg to join him. 'I ignored them when I was younger, of course—' he gave a rueful smile '—but now I try—if I become King, though—'

'There will be even more rules?' Meg offered.

'Many more.' Luca nodded. 'And running a casino conflicts with many of them. Your brother, Alessandro, would have had to give up his profession to be King—the ruler of Niroli must dedicate their life to the kingdom.'

'Alex would never give up medicine.' Meg knew that instantly. 'It's his life, but…'

'Running a casino is not so noble, huh?' Luca gave a weary shrug. 'It is not about what I want—I have been brought up to know that. When you are royalty, you know from an early age that things are different. I have always known there was a chance that one day I might be King. The fact I hoped it would never happen is irrelevant. It is what is expected, how I have been raised.'

'What does your mother say?'

'She is proud.' Luca shrugged. 'What mother wouldn't want her son to be King?'

Plenty that Meg could think of, but she didn't say that, of course, the abyss between them widening. Luca's world was just so far removed from hers, but something Luca had said didn't sit right. Meg could still hear the bitter note in Laura's voice when she'd spoken of Alex, was sure that, despite what Luca said, Laura was far from happy at the prospect of Luca ruling Niroli.

'What about your father?' Meg ventured. 'What would he have said about all this?'

'Nothing.' Luca's voice was black with bitterness. 'By this time of night he would be too drunk to form a sentence.' He gave a tight smile at her shocked expression. 'There— you have a story you can sell afterwards!'

'I would never do that. When you say—'

'Enough about me.' Luca rolled onto his side and stared over to where she sat, hugging her knees, gazing out to the ocean as she pondered his impossible life. 'Tell me something about you.'

'Like what?'

'What work do you do? Why did you leave your family to travel? As you say, I know nothing about you.'

'Me neither.' She smiled at his frown. '*That's* why I'm travelling. I work as a receptionist at a hotel in Queensland.'

'Do you enjoy it?' Luca enquired.

'Not really.' Meg shrugged. 'I like it, I suppose, the staff are nice and it pays the bills, but it's certainly not what I want to do for the rest of my life.'

'What work would you like to do?'

'I'll send you a postcard when I've worked that one out.'

'And in Australia, is there a boyfriend?' There was a

slightly hesitant note to his voice as if her answer actually mattered, but, Meg checked herself, a mere detail like that wouldn't matter to Luca. He wanted one thing and one thing only from her, and she'd better not forget it.

'No, well, no one special.'

'Has there been?' Luca asked perceptively. 'Is that what you are running away from?'

'I'm not running away,' Meg said defensively, 'and, no, there hasn't really been anyone special.'

'No children?'

'Of course not.' Meg laughed. 'I just told you I don't even have a boyfriend.'

'You never know in these times.' Luca shrugged. 'Would you like children some day?'

Meg gave a low laugh. 'Your mother told me to keep the conversation light….'

'My mother is not here.' Luca rolled his eyes. 'Well, would you?'

'I don't know.' Meg stared out into the distance—funny that the questions Luca was asking were all the ones she was asking of herself. 'Again—when I've worked out the answers I'll send you a postcard.'

He couldn't help but reach out and touch her.

Despite the closeness of their bodies, despite the conversation, as he stared at her, Luca felt as if he were watching from a distance, standing on the balcony of his apartment and watching this troubled lady sitting on the beach. Her loneliness was so palpable he wanted to end it, wanted to reach out and hold her, but as he did, as his hands reached for hers she jumped as if she'd been burnt. But Luca wasn't daunted, capturing her hand again and holding onto it, despite her resistance, feeling the pounding of her radial pulse beneath his fingers from just the tiniest contact and as slowly it settled, that troubled heart beating a more regular rhythm, Luca was filled with something akin to pride....

She *was* like a kitten. Oh, not the cute cuddly kind, more like the feral one who had come at night to the castle when he was younger, crying and meowing to be let in, then hissing and spitting when you approached.

His mother had put out scraps.

Luca could still remember her, dressed in her finest, jewels around her throat, a tiara in her hair, placing a saucer outside.

'Perché?' He could hear his youthful voice ask why? Why would she care about this tiny wild creature that didn't even want her help? Why would she come out into the cold for something so wild and ungrateful? But now he understood the rewards that came from the most unexpected of sources.

The noise of the casino, the endless demands on him had been no different from the thousands before, only today it had grated. For the first time he had actually wanted to come home, wanted to see her, *needed* to know more about her.

'I was angry at the restaurant,' Luca admitted, surprising himself with his honesty. 'Angry because all day I have looked forward to seeing you—and when I came home it was as if *you* had vanished.'

'You told me to.'

'I know....' He ran a confused hand over his forehead, intoned the words over and over. 'I know, I know...Meg, I do not know what is happening here—I just know that it cannot!'

'I know too.' Meg gulped, because she did. They were light years apart—two distant stars colliding, impossible in the present with the fallout yet to come.

'What I said—about your eating—I am very sorry. It was careless and thoughtless.'

'It was,' Meg said, then relented a touch, hearing the genuineness in his apology. 'I used to have an eating disorder. I don't actually do all that any more—I haven't in years….' She gave a pensive smile. 'You've no idea how good it feels to be able to say that.'

'You are better now?' Luca asked. 'Recovered?'

'Recovering,' Meg corrected. 'You never fully get over something like that—it's there with you always. Oh, nothing like it was—I don't panic about food all the time. I actually enjoy eating now….'

'Just not eight courses.' Luca winced.

'And not with an entire restaurant watching on!' Meg smiled at his discomfort.

'I truly am sorry,' he offered again.

'You weren't to know.'

'Can I?'

Even though his question wasn't particularly well phrased, Meg knew what he was asking and her first instinct was to change the subject, stand up perhaps and walk away….

Only she didn't.

Staring at the vast moon hanging like a paper lantern over the inky ocean, she sat in grateful silence for a moment until the flutter in her stomach stilled a touch, waited for the knee-jerk reaction to abate, and when it did Luca was waiting, patiently waiting for her to tell her story, if she so wanted.

And for the first time she did; she actually wanted to share this vital piece of herself with Luca, for no purpose or gain that she could fathom, other than that he was here—that, however unwittingly, he'd exposed her secret and that he mattered; to Meg, he mattered, *this* moment, however fleeting, really mattered. She turned and looked at him for a sliver of a second, then turned back to the beach, drinking in the view, searing it in her mind, knowing that if it ended, *when* it ended, this slice of time would be forever important.

'I was the biggest mistake of my parents' lives.' She didn't look at him as she spoke, didn't want to see his reaction, see the shock of sympathy in his eyes as she told her tale.

'Your parents?' Luca checked, watching her stiffen, then rephrasing his question. 'Your biological parents?'

'They'd never intended to have children and they never let me forget it even for a moment. They led this bohemian lifestyle, drifting from one place to another, which sounds romantic, only it wasn't….' Meg paused for a moment, arching her neck backwards and staring higher into at the sky as if searching for answers. 'I didn't fit into their lifestyle. Apparently I was a needy, very demanding baby.'

'Aren't all babies?'

'Perhaps,' Meg conceded. 'I think any demand on them from me was too much. If they hadn't had me they could have travelled more, had their all-night parties with their hippy friends—that's what they said anyway. All I know for sure is that they wanted me to disappear so in the end I did.'

'You ran away?'

'No, I just ceased to exist.'

'I don't understand.'

'You never could,' Meg said quietly. 'In all my childhood I can't remember one cuddle, not one kind word—not one,' she reiterated. 'Sometimes I wish they'd beat me—'

'Don't say that,' Luca interrupted, but Meg refused to back down.

'As I got older I tried to help them, tidying, cooking, cleaning, but nothing I did worked. All they wanted was for me to stay in my room, so in the end I did. I came out when they weren't there, used the bathroom before they got home so I wouldn't disturb them, ate whatever they'd left out for me…by the time it finished I wasn't allowed in the fridge or pantry. I was just left scraps.'

'How?'

Meg turned in surprise as he asked the question.

'How were they found out?' He frowned quizzically at her response. 'Did I say something wrong?'

'Most people ask who did I tell, or why didn't I say something…?'

'You were a child,' Luca said. 'They were your parents. How could you know it was so very wrong?'

'I didn't,' Meg sniffed, swallowing back tears, astounded by his insight, that this arrogant, seemingly insensitive man could, when it really mattered, say the very right thing. 'I just knew I felt bad, knew that my family wasn't normal, it was like this dirty secret and there was no one I could tell….'

'I know.'

Glassy eyes jerked to his, her first thought to scoff, to tell him he couldn't possibly know, but as she looked over, saw the pain in his eyes, Meg realised that he did, that somehow Luca, this royal prince, this man with the most privileged of backgrounds, somehow had visited the dark hole she was clawing her way out of.

'How *do* you know?' Meg whispered, the derision that would have been in her voice a mere few seconds ago completely absent. 'What happened, Luca?'

'It is not my tale to tell.' He shook his proud head. 'But I know what you say when you describe keeping a secret. I know how I felt in school, seeing my family in the newspaper in the morning, on the television some evenings, being told over and over how lucky, how privileged, how very noble…' He didn't finish, *couldn't*, Meg realised. Instead he asked a question of his own. 'If your parents didn't feed you, wouldn't you want food even more so now?'

'I wish!' She gave a small laugh, but it wasn't mocking, knowing no one could understand, that even she couldn't truly understand it. 'My parents *forgot* to enroll me in high school, eventually the welfare system caught up and, to cut a long story short, I was adopted by the two most wonderful people. Suddenly I had everything, parents who adored me, a brother, a beautiful home, food prepared for me… I just couldn't accept it. I kept waiting for it to all just disappear, sure that if I put a foot wrong, somehow they'd hate me too. I hit puberty, suddenly I was growing up, I suppose food was the only thing I thought I could control….'

She stopped then, utterly drained from her revelation, and even if there was loads more to say, right now she simply couldn't manage it, wondering now his take on all this. She turned shyly to face him, bracing herself for shock or sympathy in his eyes from her sorry tale, that maybe he'd parcel her off, return her from whence she came, like shop-soiled goods, but his eyes were now adoring her, his want for her never more visible, and for Meg it was a revelation. She was stunned that, after she'd given him the very worst piece of her, somehow, he considered her beautiful. And best of all he didn't try to end the conversation with trite words or well-worn clichés when none of them could have helped. Instead, reaching over, he kissed her softly, delivering a tender touch when she needed it the most.

'Come,' Luca said, pulling away, and Meg knew he was struggling, knew that the kiss they had just shared had been meant as a display of compassion, but with the energy between them it was a dangerous move. Like a match tossed onto parched bushland as he stood up and offered his hand, the whole place, Meg knew could ignite at any second; the tension as they headed towards his home was palpable.

'I am tired of staying at the palace.' It was Luca that filled the strained silence and Meg looked up at the castle and saw through his eyes, perhaps, the imposing walls that shadowed them.

'You hate it, don't you?'

'No,' Luca said wearily, 'but no matter how many times I walk this path I never feel I am going home. After the Feast we will move back to the casino,' Luca said decisively. 'There I can relax.'

'Why?' She knew she was pushing, knew she was asking more than he was prepared to give, but still she persisted, guilty almost at having revealed so much of herself, needing him to do the same. 'Why doesn't it feel like—?'

'Leave it, Meg,' Luca growled, his hand tight around hers, but just as he warned her away he let her come a little closer, slowing the pace till finally they stood facing each other. 'I never feel like I belong there—it is hard to explain. I am told I was born to all this and yet sometimes I feel like a stranger… Enough!' He walked on more purposefully now, letting go of her hand as she went to retrieve her shoes, and she wished she knew what to say, wished she knew the questions to ask, but instead she concentrated on the tiny buckles of her sandals, her hand shaking so much she could barely manage the simple task, so conscious now of his presence. When she stood she knew he'd be there waiting, knew they wouldn't be walking a step further.

'Oh, Meg…' Luca's lips crushed hers as his hungry mouth sought hers. This wasn't anything like the kiss they had shared back at the casino. That had been about lust and attraction; this one was more, so much more.

It ached of need, of want, of something she had never felt, his kiss so overwhelming, so demanding, so consuming that it was all she could think of, all she wanted to think of. Kissing off her lipstick, devouring her, he was pushing her down onto the sand, yet supporting her at the same time, her body sinking backwards as somehow he broke her fall, lowering her onto the sandy floor, his body on top of her, the weight of him exquisite, the *feel* of him pressing into her, wedging her beneath him. His hands dragged over her, his fingers pressing into her breast, searching for the side zipper and locating it, moaning as his fingers met her warm, ripe flesh, and to an onlooker it would have looked like an attack, but the apparent suddenness, the haste, was a mirage. It had been building since he'd come home, since their first kiss, since they'd laid eyes on each other, and Meg knew he somehow needed this, that whatever dark place he'd just visited in his mind, this was what he needed to chase it away, and she gave it to him gladly, gave it because she needed it, too.

Needed to escape for a moment as well.

His rough jaw scratched at her chest, his mouth searching and claiming her nipple, sucking her sweet flesh as his hands slid up her dress, cupping her bottom, his erection pressing against the satin of her knickers and she wanted him.

Wanted him.

Meg's body was responding without her orders, bold in a way she'd never been before. As he slid down his own zipper, her hips lifted to welcome him, his manhood still pressing into her knickers as she slid provocatively beneath him, rueing the strip of satin that parted them, losing herself in the delicious friction. His needy fingers were tearing at the flimsy material and, panting with expectancy, she knew the second he tore them free he would be inside her, knew from his rasping breath, his jerking motions, that he was as close as her, and the first flicker of Meg's orgasm was aligning, at the greedy thought of him spilling as he entered her....

'I have wanted this—' as he tore off her knickers Luca's arbitrary words were those of a lover in the throes of passion '—since I first saw you. This, this is what I wanted.'

Sex.

This wasn't the deal they had struck—sex, yes, but not this! Not this wild abandonment, not giving herself to him so completely, so fully, letting him take such supreme control, and something in her died, the motions purely mechanical now as Luca positioned himself to enter her. But he pulled back, his voice hoarse with question as he sensed the rapid change in her, felt the body that had been so closely meshed with his unyielding now in his arms. 'What is wrong?'

'Nothing,' she whispered, closing her eyes, willing the moment over, wanting him to just take her and be done, but that wasn't enough for Luca. He'd tasted her fervour and wanted more, his confused eyes searching hers for an answer.

'What just happened there?'

'Nothing,' she attempted, tried to pretend that everything was okay, but the passion of before wasn't one that could be manufactured, the sheer assault of emotion that had hit her not one that could be faked, and Luca knew it.

'One minute you are alive in my arms, one minute you are crying out my name, then this! I need to know what happened, Meg.'

'I changed my mind!' Embarrassed, confused, she found

it was easier to shout than cry, easier to attack than back down. 'I am allowed to, you know.'

'You really should be more careful how you tease men.'

'I wasn't teasing....' Tears were threatening but she gulped them back, Luca's brutal response stinging with each sharp word.

'Much more careful!' he reiterated loudly. 'When I met you, you were accepting drinks off rich businessmen—I should have known better.'

'I'm not like that,' Meg insisted, but Luca wasn't to be swayed by her pleas.

'Aren't you?' he demanded. 'Well, if you're really not then here's a piece of advice: lying on a beach half naked with your legs wrapped around me is not the wisest time to change your mind. Not all men are as honourable as me!'

'I know.' Her teeth were chattering so violently she could barely get the words out. He had every right to be angry, every right to be confused; Meg was herself. It wasn't sex that was the problem, it was the feelings behind the act—how could she possibly tell him it was *how* much she wanted him that scared her the most? 'Maybe we should just...' Her mind searched for answers and desperate times called for desperate measures, and not all of them wise. Leaning forward, she pressed her mouth to his, kissed him with all the false passion she could mount, screwing her eyes closed in shame and mortification as with an enraged howl he pushed her aside.

'Get it over with!' He finished the unspoken sentence for her, and added his own crude twist to the end. 'Do it like dogs in the street then walk away. I am a prince!' Angry, dignified and straight to the point, he stood up and arranged his clothing as Meg did the same. 'I have absolutely no need to accept your charity.'

CHAPTER TEN

THE TENSION had been unbearable since they'd returned.

Luca, refusing to spend two nights on the sofa, had thrown her out a blanket and one of her very new nightdresses, then commandeered the royal bed, clearly with no expectation of her joining him, and Meg had spent the night staring into the dying embers of the fire.

She wanted him.

More times through the night than she could remember she'd stood up, wanting so badly to go into his room, to explain that her change in mood had been nothing to do with him and everything to do with her, but she'd baulked at the final hurdle. Hand gripping the door handle, ready to knock, over and over she'd padded back to the couch.

'I am late!' Bristling with rancour, Luca stalked into the lounge dressed in nothing but black boxer shorts and a foul mood. Picking up the phone and demanding coffee, he turned his angry mood back to her when she tried to talk to him.

'Luca, about last night…'

'There's nothing to discuss,' Luca dismissed, 'and could you please at least put on a robe? Don't display what's not for sale, Meg.'

'You put out this nightdress for me, Luca,' Meg argued. 'What else was I supposed to wear? I'm not trying to tease you. I'm trying to talk to you!'

'I don't need to hear it,' Luca roared. 'Since the moment I set eyes on you, you have caused nothing but trouble—reeling me in with your lies, with your sob stories. Well, not any more. Now you are in my palace and you will act by my rules.' He disappeared for a moment, then came over, stood over her, his black eyes filled with contempt as he picked up her arm as if she were a belligerent child, dressing her in a robe and bundling her onto the sofa. 'For two more days you are in Niroli—and then, I want you out of here.'

'Fine!' Meg snapped—and it should have been. He wasn't sending her back to prison. In two days she would be out of here, and clearly from Luca's reaction he didn't expect her to sleep with him now. She'd got exactly what she wanted—so why did she feel like crying?

'Now I must go to mass—I am expected to go at Feast weekend.'

'Do I have to come?'

'Please,' Luca snorted. 'Only a lady would join me at mass, only a woman who was considered suitable to be my wife would come with me—and you, Meg, are neither. This morning, apart from the staff you will have the palace much to yourself—the family will be at various celebrations for the Feast. This afternoon you will make full use of the staff that come from the spa to do your hair and make-up, and then you will escort me to the ball tonight.'

'I'm surprised you'd want me to,' Meg bit back, close to crying and trying not to let him see.

'The place settings are done—your name is already down, I need an escort and I have neither the time nor inclination to find another. You will be there with me.' A knock at the door heralding the arrival of his coffee didn't stop his sharp tongue. 'I can bring any tart to that!'

She was tempted to stay in the room after he'd left, to just hide herself away, but his acrid words played over and over in her mind and in the end Meg was grateful to leave the apartment for a while. She found herself walking along the marble corridors; the staff were everywhere, busy arranging vast floral arrangements, polishing the marble floors, giving her curious looks as she passed. Meg felt like an intruder and a fraud. As if she'd been locked in some luxurious department store— all the treasures on show, but nothing she could ever own.

'Can I get you anything, *signorina?*' One of the maids approached as Meg stood gazing out at the sparkling pool and, because she was in a palace, because incidentals like heading back to her room to collect the new bathers she'd chosen yesterday didn't matter here, Meg, for the first time, utilised her temporary privileged position.

'I'd like to swim.'

'Of course.' The maid smiled. 'I'll send someone to collect your things—this way.' She led Meg through to the changing room. In a matter of minutes the small gold-thread bikini she had chosen had arrived. And by the time Meg had stepped out poolside, a jug of iced lemonade and a fruit platter were waiting for her.

'If you need anything else just pick up the phone.'

'I won't,' Meg said, thanking her.

The bliss of the cool water on her body was unsurpassed. Sliding through the still, azure pool, she found it was easy to forget the turmoil of her life, the chaos that had brought her to this point, but real life soon invaded. The maid's white shoes were waiting for her as she breathlessly came to the edge and, squinting into the sunlight, Meg shielded her eyes and looked up as the maid informed her that a visitor had arrived for her at the palace.

'Who?' Meg asked, her mind galloping hopefully—a lawyer, perhaps, or even Alex—frowning when she heard who it was.

'Jasmine—she says she is a close friend. Would you like Security to let her through the gates?'

'Jasmine?'

It seemed a decade since she'd seen Jasmine, so much had happened since that night at the casino, and Meg's heart soared—finally someone who could help her sort this mess out. Finally someone who would be able to help her clear her name.

CHAPTER ELEVEN

ACID CHURNED in his stomach.

For Luca, disgustingly healthy with the constitution of an ox, the overwhelming nausea that struck him as he left the church was an enigma. The blistering sun on the white tomb-stones was too bright this morning, the noise from the jubilant crowd just too loud. Despite the heat of the morning, the sweat that broke on his brow was icy cold. For a moment, as he excused himself, put on dark shades and darted around the side of the building, he thought he must have food poisoning.

'*Ke che*, Luca?'

It was his mother, her face etched with concern, her hands reaching up to pull off the dark glasses and try to fathom what was wrong.

'*Dove* Meg?' As direct as her son, she asked Meg's where-abouts, frowning as Luca gave a casual shrug. 'Why didn't you bring her with you?'

'Why *would* I bring her here?'

'Because she is Alessandro's sister,' Laura answered carefully.

'She is not his blood.' Luca shrugged. 'It is up to the king to introduce her if he sees fit. Anyway, she is just visiting Niroli for a few days; it's no big deal.'

'That's not how it seemed to me yesterday.' Laura frowned up at her son. 'Yesterday you asked me to take care of her, to look after her as if she were family. I got the distinct impression you like her.'

'She is just a girl, just a woman I met a couple of days ago. If I bring her here to the church…' He gestured to the crowds of well-wishers, waiting for a glimpse of their beloved royal family, the press with their cameras ready, all descending on Niroli in expectation of the grand ball to be held tonight.

'People might think it is serious?' Laura finished for him.

'Exactly.' Luca nodded, glad that his mother got it. 'It would be all over the papers tomorrow.'

'You have to live, Luca.' Laura pointed out. 'The press are always going to jump to conclusions, whatever you do or don't do—they will make their own story. You know how it is.'

'Meg doesn't, though.' Luca shook his head. 'I don't think she'd…' He gave a helpless gesture with his hands. 'She is not like most other women; she would not like the scrutiny.'

'So you want to protect her?' Laura asked softly, her knowing eyes taking in the grim set of her son's mouth.

'It's not that simple.' Luca gave an impatient shake of his head, but Laura wasn't to be deterred. Despite the dark glasses, despite the sheer height of him, Laura confronted him, tried to get him to express the problem.

'Feelings never are, Luca.' She put a hand to his arm. 'This is the first time I have heard you talk about a woman like this, the first time I have seen you worrying about what the press might do to her. I would say that Meg is *not like most women* in more ways than one for you.'

She was.

Meg wasn't like most women he had dated, in fact Meg wasn't like any woman he had ever met.

She was *more* of a woman—as if the essence of femininity had somehow been distilled, the mere scent of her provoking a need, a want, that was unsurpassed—yet she enraged him.

Her carelessness with herself, her recklessness—his anger at her this morning had been more at himself than at her. How could he explain to his mother—to anyone—that the woman back at the palace had stolen, not only the Niroli jewels, but his heart as well?

Dio, what did this woman do to him?

'It does not matter how I feel.' Still Luca resisted the temptation; still he refused to fathom the possibility. 'She leaves on Tuesday anyway.'

'Then talk to her now, Luca,' Laura urged. 'Spend time with her while you have it.'

'I have things to do today.' Luca shook his head at the hopelessness of it all. 'Commitments, you know that.'

'You will always have commitments, Luca,' Laura answered hotly. 'As long as you are a prince, duty will always be calling you, and if you become King—' She took a deep breath and steadied herself because no elaboration was needed; they both knew what lay ahead if that was the path laid out for him. 'You must learn balance—' her voice was softer, but no less urgent '—to survive in this family; sometimes your first duty must be to yourself.'

'Yours never was.' Seeing the warning look in his mother's eyes, Luca snapped his mouth closed and gritted his teeth—the subject he had touched on was still barred after all these years, but the churning feeling in his stomach was back, the *rage* he felt rising again, and for the first time ever, he had his say.

'I saw what that bastard did to you.' As his mother opened her mouth to protest, to shush him, Luca overrode her.

'Don't ask me to be quiet again. Don't tell me I have no idea what I'm talking about.'

'This is surely not the place, Luca.'

'Where is?' Luca continued. 'Back at the palace in front of the staff, or maybe we should go to the local Niroli psychologist.'

'Luca, please…' Laura begged, but he was beyond reason.

'I tried to help you! After, when I came to see if you were okay, you slapped me, you told me I spoke filthy lies, that I imagined things. But what sort of sick person would make that up?'

'Luca, you didn't make it up…' Tears spilled out of his mother's well-made-up eyes. 'I am so sorry I confused you, slapped you… Can you understand that I was trying to protect you?'

'How?' The noise from the gathered crowd, cheering as the royal family left the church, drowned out his wounded roar, the Niroli church bells peeling out to celebrate the Feast as Luca raged at the world he had witnessed as a child. 'How can you say you were protecting me, by denying what I know I saw?' He thought he might actually vomit, right there at her feet as the filth of the past spilled out. 'He beat you, slammed his fist into your face over and over. I saw him kicking you, beating you—that man was my father who I was supposed to respect and obey. That bastard would have been King. Where do the Niroli Rules apply here, Mother? Where was his honour when he did that to you?'

'Don't be angry, Luca,' Laura pleaded. 'Let it pass—let it rest now. He is gone.'

'Yet still you defend him,' Luca croaked, still breaking the rules, stepping in territory that was as forbidden as it was new. 'By pretending you were happy, by pretending you had choices, he is not gone—still he is here, still he has the power over you.' He almost expected to be slapped—for her hand to silence him again just as it had all those years ago, the one time he'd confronted her—and again he'd have taken it, for his mother he'd have taken it, but instead he was stunned to see that through her tears she was smiling; a soft, pensive smile that only confused him.

'I *was* happy, Luca.'

'How?'

'I took the advice I just gave you—I learnt balance. I learnt that, to survive, sometimes my first duty was to myself. Luca, what happened was wrong, but that is not the entire picture— it is not *all* that our marriage was. Let your father rest, Luca. Don't waste your life hating what you cannot change.'

'Is that what you did?'

She didn't need to answer, the answer was there for him to see—and even if he didn't understand, he accepted it, believed it, because for the first time he looked, really looked at his mother—saw the serenity in her face that surely only came when one was truly at peace with themselves—and he saw what was missing in Meg.

'I have been told by the king there is to be no more scandal.' Luca dragged in a breath, wondered whether to go on, but the honesty of before had forged a new path and, after a moment's hesitation, Luca continued to lead the way, a tiny smile twisting his tense mouth as he tried to sum up Meg to his mother. 'She is trouble!'

'You were trouble,' Laura pointed out. 'And if this Meg were straightforward she would not hold your interest for long, Luca.' Laura smiled too, revelling in the new closeness, even managing a small joke of her own. 'Then you'd end up getting divorced and what a scandal that would be—better to get it over with now, perhaps? The people of Niroli can forgive an honest mistake.'

'What about a dishonest one?' Luca watched as his mother winced, but she quickly recovered.

'Talk to your lady, Luca—whatever the problem, surely you, of all people, can work it out.'

Maybe he could.

Driving back to the palace, Luca was filled with possibility. He had paid the guard off—that drunk wouldn't remember anything anyway, would never put the two women together. Despite what he'd told her, Meg didn't need a lawyer—her things were in the boot of his car. Pulling over, he ripped open the backpack—her passport, her clothes were all there, and he would offer her them now, give her the chance to leave the island if that was what she wanted—but first he'd ask her to stay.

The magnitude of what he was proposing to do dawned on Luca then—she was a liar, a thief, a commoner and clearly she had issues. She was the last person a prince, a future king should be dating, but then again…

Picking up the sheer top she had worn that fateful night, remembering the feel of her in his arms, the *instant* attraction that had propelled them—forced them—to this point, Luca realised she was the *only* person he could be dating, that whatever her problems, whatever had happened in the past, he wanted to help her, to release her from whatever prison she was in.

Burying his face in the soft silk, Luca knew he could no more walk away now than he could have done when he'd found her in the cell.

Taking a deep breath, he closed his eyes in expectation, waiting for the heady, feminine fragrance that was so much Meg to drench his senses, frowning at the cheap, musky scent that filled his nostrils.

Unfurling the top in his hand, he noticed the wine and food stains on the delicate fabric—realising then the horrendous mistake he had made in not trusting her!

And for the first time in the whole sorry saga he cried.

CHAPTER TWELVE

'SURELY HE MUST have given you some money?' Jasmine's voice was angry and desperate as she refused over and over to accept that Meg could give her nothing. Since the moment she'd teetered to the poolside, hung-over and bitter, Meg had realised it was a mistake to have let her in.

One of the maids was cleaning nearby windows, frowning at the disturbance by the pool, Jasmine's greedy requests getting louder by the minute, her anger escalating, the situation rapidly getting out of control.

'I think you should leave now, Jasmine.' Meg tried to keep her voice controlled and even, tried not to show the anxiety she was feeling as her supposed friend overstepped all the boundaries.

'Why?' Jasmine shouted. 'Are you worried that I'll embarrass you in front of your new posh friends? You didn't mind me when I was getting drinks bought for us all night, did you?' She was walking over now and Meg blanched at the stench of stale alcohol on her breath, knew that at any minute Jasmine might even hit her, and that there was absolutely nothing she could do except suffer the indignity of a so-called cat fight in Luca's beautiful home.

'I think you've outstayed your welcome, Jasmine.'

It wasn't just Luca's unexpected presence that had Meg jumping, but the absolute loathing in his voice and, despite their row and the harsh words that had been uttered just a couple of hours ago, she'd never been so relieved to see him. Jasmine was out of control and things were turning nasty, but so commanding was Luca's presence that within seconds Jasmine had picked up her bag.

'I was just leaving!'

'I didn't mean just here at the palace.' As Jasmine flounced off, the thunder of Luca's voice momentarily stopped her in her tracks. 'I want you out of Niroli.'

'Luca!' Despite her relief that the situation was under control, Meg thought he was being a bit harsh by demanding Jasmine leave the island, but clearly, whatever Meg thought, she actually knew nothing, because suddenly Jasmine was running, her stilettos not the ideal footwear for a quick poolside getaway, but Luca didn't chase her. He didn't move an inch, just stood as two of his bodyguards caught the woman in a rather undignified tussle.

'What's going on?' Meg begged, startled eyes turning to Luca, then widening in horror as realisation dawned even before Luca had a chance to explain.

'Your *friend* was the thief.' Luca's lips sneered the words out as he glared over at Jasmine. 'Your *friend* borrowed your top when she sobered up and realised how *stupido* she'd been to attempt to steal from the Fierezzas she decided to get rid of the evidence—in your bag!" He didn't await Meg's reaction, just strode along the pool to where Jasmine stood, her drunken bravado gone in the face of such power, Luca clearly someone no one would choose to mess with. 'My staff will take you to the port and see you onto a boat. If you choose to stay, then that is your right, but know I will press charges. I will use all my might, and, believe me, it is plenty, to see that you are prosecuted to the full extent of the law. My family writes the rules of Niroli, Jasmine, and I will make it my business to see that they are followed to the letter!'

'How?' Meg was sitting on the bed in her bikini, still trembling from the vile confrontation with Jasmine, and reeling from the shock of Luca's revelation. Still burning from his horribly hurtful words to her this morning. 'How did you know? Have you always known it was her?'

'I found out about ten minutes before you did.' Luca sat down beside her, went to put an arm around her to comfort her, to stop her shaking, but Meg brushed him off. Feigned affection was not what she needed now. 'I am sorry for not believing you.'

'I presume I'm free to go.' It wasn't a question, but a statement. Meg stood on rather shaky legs and tried to locate her robe, suddenly conscious of her lack of attire.

'Your things are in my car.' Luca couldn't look at her, actually had to divert his eyes. To see her so stunned and still so very proud, to see that gorgeous body barely dressed and know he had no claim on it was killing him inside, and because it was a morning for being honest, and lies had got him nowhere, he told Meg the full truth. 'They have always been in my car. The night I came to the jail—I didn't pay your bail. I bribed the guard. There were no charges being laid, no need for you to contact a lawyer—'

'There was no need for me to be here at all really,' Meg bitterly broke in, fruitlessly searching for the blessed robe as she digested his words, not realising she'd left it down at the pool. 'You didn't even get sex!'

'I don't want sex from you, Meg,' Luca said wearily.

'Well, if you've quite finished completely humiliating me, could you possibly arrange to get my things sent up from the car and then I'll be out of here?'

He found his *own* robe for her, handed it to her, summoning the strength to say what he felt as she put it on. It was way too big for her, smothering her slender body, her hands trembling with fury and indignation as she did up the tie.

'I want you to stay, Meg.'

'Why?' she snapped. 'Now I'm not a common thief I'm suddenly more acceptable? Well, guess what, Luca—nothing's actually changed. I never was a thief, I never deserved to be spoken to in the way you did before—'

'I understand that,' Luca interrupted. 'And this has nothing to do with what I have just found out—even before I realised Jasmine was the thief I was on my way home to ask you to stay.'

She didn't buy it, just didn't get it, shaking her head as he surely heaped lie upon lie. 'Would you please just get my things?'

'Only when you listen to me.' Luca was talking over her now. 'Only when you hear what I have to say.'

'There's nothing *to* say,' Meg interrupted furiously. 'You've kept me a virtual prisoner here—'

'I understand you have been treated badly...' His accent was thick with emotion. 'And I also now understand why you did not want to sleep with me; without trust it is nothing.' The directness of his statement silenced her, silenced even Luca for a moment, honesty a breath away and both terrified to hear it, scared of saying the wrong thing, of blowing out the tiny flicker that still existed between them. 'You gave me all of you—told me about yourself, asked me to believe in you—yet I gave you *nothing* in return. I do not want just sex from you, Meg, I want the passion, I want the woman I held in my arms before, I want you crying out my name because you need to hear it—and I understand now why you felt you could not give that piece of yourself.'

'I just wanted you to trust me.'

'I know,' Luca said softly. 'And for that I will always be sorry, but will you believe me when I say that through it all I never stopped trusting *in* you?'

'That doesn't make sense.' Meg frowned, trying to work out the translation, but this time Luca hadn't made a mistake.

'Always I have trusted in you. Trusted that you were a better person than the one I was seeing, trusted that there was more to you than the woman that was being revealed to me.'

He had. With blinding clarity, Meg saw that, despite everything, *always* he had been there for her—always he had believed that she could be so much better. He just hadn't known that she already was.

'You asked that night in the restaurant what I wanted you to be. Had I not made that stupid comment you would have heard my answer—what I wanted was the you I knew was in there. Somewhere between the grubby little thief I first brought home, and the polished mannequin I took out that night. *That*, I believe, is the real Meg, the one I was desperate, *am* desperate, to get to know—if you'll let me.'

She didn't know how to respond, so he did it for her.

'I understand this is a lot to take in. I just ask that you do not leave in haste.'

'You have to go…' Confused, she shook her head. 'You have the parade, duties to attend.'

'They can wait,' Luca said firmly.

'The king said there must be no more scandal.' She

actually wanted him to leave, wanted some time alone to draw breath, to assimilate her jumbled thoughts into some sort of order, to process all that he was saying. 'You can't just let everyone down….' She was fumbling for excuses. At this, the most important moment in her life, she was practically throwing him out, pointing out why he couldn't possibly stay, and Luca saw through her in an instant.

'Do you want me to leave, Meg?'

'No.' Like a driver swerving to avoid a child, her first reaction was pure instinct, but as she slammed her foot on the brakes it was about slowing things down, avoiding the impact that was surely inevitable. 'Yes, I think you should….'

'What is wrong, Meg? And don't say nothing.'

'I'm scared,' she admitted, watching his aghast expression. 'Not of you—of me. Luca…' Shy yet brave, she told him her truth. 'Last night, when I stopped, when you thought I was teasing…'

'You don't have to explain.'

'But I do.' Meg gulped. 'I wanted you the first night I met you and every minute since. I want you so much it scares me.'

'You have never slept with anyone?' Luca asked, confused when she shook her head.

'I have, but not like that.' Her eyes pleaded with him to understand. 'Luca, when I'm with you…it's like I lose it, like I have no control.'

'That is what lovemaking is—trusting in each other's bodies, losing your mind, your control and knowing no harm will come. In my arms you would be safe.'

'I don't think I can,' Meg whispered. 'I don't think I can be the woman you want…'

'You already are,' Luca said. 'And one day, you will want

me as I want you, one day you will be ready to trust me—till then I wait.'

He didn't have to—that he understood her fear, that still he stood before her, not judging, just understanding, made her safe, made her sure, and it was Meg now reaching out for him, made bold by his certainty, by his utter faith in all that they could be.

'It doesn't have to be now,' he said.

'Oh, it does,' Meg whispered.

'You want it quickly over and done with?' Luca teased, just enough to eke out a smile. 'I'm sure that can be easily arranged!' But the joking was over then—her honest admission tearing at his heartstrings.

'I don't want to let you down,' she said quietly.

'You never, ever could.'

Tentatively he kissed her and she felt his tender restraint, his hand warming her shivering body, the scent of chlorine mingling with his cologne, and though it had none of the urgency of before, it was so loaded with passion, so full of a deeper desire, it could only gain in momentum.

Her momentum.

Suddenly she was aware of her near nakedness compared to him, instead of being embarrassing, it irritated her. She needed to feel his skin against hers, her impatient hands fiddling with his shirt buttons until Luca halted her.

'Enjoy the journey,' Luca whispered, removing her hands and taking off his own shirt, his own clothes as still he kissed her. 'There is no rush.'

Oh, but there was.

Some people looked better dressed, but not Luca—stunning in a suit, he was absolutely breathtaking naked. Every promise she had glimpsed replayed tenfold when she saw him—exquisitely beautiful, like the Statue of David she had taken her camera to on her trip to Rome, his shoulders wide, a fan of jet hair on his broad chest all tapering to a flat, toned stomach. Until that moment, Meg hadn't thought men's legs could be sexy, only his were. His muscular thighs glimmered. And because she could, because she should, Meg glimpsed the bit that mattered, history rewritten as she defined true masculine beauty—the Statue of David way out of proportion to this Adonis.

Maybe he sensed the shift in her, maybe her fervour was infectious, because it was Luca now calling the shots, his thick arms pulling her towards him, fingers plying her swollen bosom from her bikini top, and then untying the laces of her bottoms, his fingers finding her swollen bud, his tongue dragging from her chest to her stomach, burying his face in her most intimate place, his tongue cooling the heat that flared and simultaneously fanning it.

She could feel her body giving in to him, feel great waves of lust ripping through her, but rather than scaring her it excited her now—as he lay her on the bed her whole body trembled with want, each kiss more intoxicating than the last, his fingers sliding into her, oiling his delicate way, till she was so moist, so ready, there was no fear, just want. The feel of him entering her, inside her, moving within her, was unsurpassed, his skin sliding against hers, his mouth kissing the hollows of her neck. She could have stayed in this moment forever, enjoying the journey as Luca had said, but her body was hurtling towards a new destination, moving to a rhythm of its own, lifting, rocking herself against him, her toes literally curling, her neck arching at the intensity of it all, and for a single second she fought it, tried to hold onto that piece of herself as his body demanded it *all*.

'Let it happen, *mia cara*,' he rasped, and so she did, and realised with shameless delight that it was Luca who was struggling to stay in control—that her body, the one she had so bitterly loathed, was utterly adored. Heat flared inside, rushing up her spine like an electric shock, her whole body stiffening, contracting, dragging him ever deeper inside. She cried out his name as Luca did hers—feeling him bucking inside her, delivering his precious load to her deprived body, and, when it was over, when her body came to a shuddering, exhausted halt, still he was holding her, still he was there, her world a little different now but surely better for what she had achieved.

For what *they* had achieved.

'I never knew it could be that good.' Meg sighed. 'Never imagined it could be so…'

'Neither did I.'

She blinked back at him—his heartfelt words were like blossoms falling, each one paving the way for the fruit that might follow, only Luca hadn't finished yet, offering now the piece of himself he had held back forever, his torrid secret somehow turned into a precious gift.

'I never knew I could want so much to share with another person—but now it is my turn to give that piece of me to you.

'I witnessed my father…' He struggled to continue only he didn't have to, Meg put her hand up to halt him.

'You don't have to tell me, Luca.'

'I want to.' Luca nodded, the gesture more for his benefit than hers, forcing a certainty that wasn't there in his voice. 'He beat her—badly. I saw it happen once when I was a child.'

'It must have been awful.'

'What was more awful was that it didn't happen.' He saw the cloud of confusion pass over her features, infinitely grateful when she didn't speak, just let him explain in his own time. 'I was told I imagined it, that my father was a wonderful man, might one day be King, how could I dare even *think* such things. My mother slapped me when I tried to help.'

It was as if she'd shaken a snow globe, those strong, arrogant features blurring, those knowing eyes clouding at the painful memory, and Meg knew better than to talk, she just held him until the blizzard settled and the features she knew aligned into focus.

'My mother told me I was never to speak of it—that it would cause more damage if anyone knew; that she could handle it. Maybe she was right—truly, I do not know. It happened since they were married. I saw photos of their honeymoon, my mother had a cut over her eye. To this day she swears she had too much wine with supper and tripped on the deck of the royal yacht.'

'Maybe she did?'

Luca gave a hollow laugh utterly void of humour. 'My father often talked of her drinking, her clumsiness, the staff did too. I guess it's easier to question the morals of the wife than those of the heir to the throne. You know, I have never seen my mother have more than one drink to be polite at a function; the clumsiness stopped the day my father died.'

'That's why you went off the rails when you were younger,' Meg offered. 'If a possible future King of Niroli could act like that, then what the hell?'

He smiled. Painful and loaded it might be, but Luca actually smiled, holding her hand back now.

'How did a little thing like you get so wise?'

'Group Therapy.' Meg even laughed as she said it. 'And a lot of it—I've heard tales that would make your hair curl.'

'Always in my life there have been duties, obligations, and for a long time I chose to ignore them.'

'But not now?' Meg ventured.

'Now I respect them,' Luca offered. 'Now I see that the rules I once snubbed, the laws I rebelled against, are actually there for a reason. To rule Niroli it is not enough to merely live by the laws of the land—a king has to live beyond them, adhere to a strict code of conduct, not just for his peoples' sake but for himself and the people he loves.

'Over and over the subjects of Niroli have forgiven me—"he is young, a little wild" —but now the excuses run out. Now I have to make a choice.' Black, agonised eyes found hers.

'Do you want to be King?'

'I don't know.' For the first time ever he sounded confused—this beautiful, strong man actually bewildered. 'You said on the beach you couldn't do it…'

'This isn't about me,' Meg urged, but it fell on deaf ears, Luca hushing her so that he could continue.

'All I know is this—you matter. You matter more to me than I can even understand. For the first time I think of someone else first. I have known you such a short time yet I feel as if you are a part of me. Does that sound mad?'

'Yes—' Meg smiled through her tears '—but, then again, I think I'm going crazy too. Luca, I cannot be a part of your decision.'

'If we stay together, Meg, if I become King, this *will* be your life—this is what you have to understand.'

'We don't have to make any choices now,' Meg insisted, but she could hear the fruitlessness of her words. As he'd explained on the first night, his status didn't allow the luxury of normal dating, and whether their relationship lasted a week or a lifetime, from the moment they stepped out together *everything* would change.

'You've been through so much.' His own torrid memories were pushed aside, his hand reached out and captured her cheek, and it was so tender, so filled with understanding. Meg rested her head in his palm, for the first time really let someone take the weight from her shoulders. 'I'm scared of what it would do to you.' His statement was as confronting as it was honest. 'The scrutiny, the constant glare of the spotlight…'

'I'm not some fragile flower, Luca.'

'You are to me,' he said softly. 'You are beautiful and precious and delicate. Meg, I have been brought up with this, yet still, sometimes when I read the papers, whether it is lies or truth that they print, it is as if acid is being thrown in my face.'

'I could handle it,' Meg insisted.

'All of it?' Luca softly checked. 'Your family, your friends, your past all fodder…' He watched as she winced, as that strong, proud face disintegrated under the weight of truth.

'I don't know,' Meg admitted.

'Then we find out,' Luca said decisively. 'Tonight we see how hot the water is.'

'Sorry?' Meg frowned, then actually managed a small laugh. 'You mean we *test* the water!'

'I prefer my own version,' Luca answered. 'Tonight you come with me.'

'As your tart?' Meg threw back his earlier statement, taking some solace in his visible wince, but Luca quickly recovered.

'Your language needs some serious work,' Luca teased, 'but, no. I am not just asking you to escort me at the ball— I am asking you to come with me.'

'There's a difference?' Meg frowned.

'A big one.' Luca stared back at her. 'Tonight I ask that you join me on the palace steps.'

'Isn't a bit... Wait a minute...
well one... face could have if her friends can that
because... makes step matter'

CHAPTER THIRTEEN

'READY?' LUCA'S soft knocking on the bathroom door, though expected, still made Meg jump. The prospect of the ball and facing Luca's relatives, the people of Niroli, were all such alien territory, she could have spent a year preparing and still it would be too soon.

Luca had been obliged to go out in the afternoon, greeting some of the more prominent dignitaries as they arrived at the tiny Niroli airport, leaving Meg at the disposal of a myriad staff—their expressive Italian voices becoming more gleeful as, bit by bit, they transformed her into a date worthy of Prince Luca Fierezza on such an important night for Niroli.

Like a prize racehorse being prepared for a race, her body had been buffed and polished so that every inch of exposed flesh glowed with healthy vitality. Her thick straight hair was coiled into a million tiny glossy ringlets and piled high on her head, but the seemingly effortless cascade that escaped had, in fact, been painstakingly cajoled into place then vigorously pinned.

And as for her make-up!

Her complexion was flawless, her teeth whiter somehow behind her glossy lips, her blue eyes so enhanced by the smoky-grey eye shadow that to Meg it looked as if she were wearing coloured contact lenses. Even her toes were unrecognisable—Meg glanced down at her polished nails peeking out of the most exquisite bejewelled, impossibly high sandals. Her body was draped in a soft taupe velvet gown, ruched at the bust; it was so well tailored it made Meg's waist impossibly small.

Staring into the mirror, this time Meg actually smiled at her reflection, somehow recognised herself beneath the glamour and hype. Unlike before, Meg had used her voice, told the dressers and make-up artists the colours she preferred, the ideas *she* had for her hair—and now she gazed in awe at the transformation.

She stared at the Meg that Luca had always known was there.

But as Luca knocked and gently summoned her, though there was nothing to touch up, nothing to fiddle with, she hesitated before stepping out, knowing that tonight she wasn't just escorting Luca to the ball, but possibly entering his future…stepping into a world that was so impossibly different and wondering if she had what it took.

He answered her question without speaking—his eyes telling her with certainty that, not only was he proud to be by her side tonight, but he knew she was nervous, promising her with the most tender of embraces that he would be there for her through it all.

'You look stunning,' he affirmed. 'Everyone is going to love you.'

'You don't look too bad yourself.' Nerves were forgotten for a moment as she glimpsed her *date*, almost had to pinch herself to believe that she was with him.

Always immaculate, always beautiful, tonight he was breathtaking. His hair was swept back off his face, making him look even more haughty, more aloof if that were possible, his exquisitely tailored suit just divine, accenting his broad shoulders, his heavy silk cravat beautifully knotted, and for once he was cleanly shaven, his skin flawless. His mouth was full and completely kissable, so she did, and her expertly applied make-up was happily forgotten as her lips met his, Luca's expert touch delivering all the confidence she needed to face the night.

'We must go....' Reluctantly Luca pulled back a touch, his arms still around her waist, encircling her, holding her exactly where she wanted to be. 'But first...'

'Can we?' Meg broke in, with all the enthusiasm of a child with a brand-new toy, sure she would never, ever be able to get enough of him! Their lovemaking was an utter revelation. She felt as if she'd spent her life with the wrong set of keys, every door, every lock a challenge—until this afternoon, until Luca had produced the master key and let her into a world she'd barely glimpsed! Showing her over and over the delights of her own body, showing her over and over the magic of his.

'You are incorrigible.' Luca laughed. 'I wasn't actually talking about making love.'

'Oh.' Meg pouted as still he held her.

'There will be time for that later; anyway...' seeing her crestfallen face, Luca made a joke '...you would ruin my hair.'

'This won't, though.'

She couldn't believe her own boldness, her own assuredness in his want for her—but heard his gasp of delighted shock as she sank to her knees. For Meg it made her impromptu decision the right one—*this* was how she could be; *this* was how she was with his trust... She took him in her mouth and all Luca could do was take what she gave him so willingly, couldn't offer a protest against something so divine, couldn't even coil his fingers in her carefully styled hair, just stood to rapid attention, his moans of pleasure shuddering into one long sigh as she completed her delicate task.

Stunned, incredulous but eternally grateful, he pulled her to her feet.

'You are a bad girl,' he attempted to scold, but his eyes were smiling.

'You'd better get used to it, then!'

Meg's first walk on the wild side put them impossibly behind schedule, of course, and by the time they *finally* made it to the door, they were already late. Luigi knocked to check that everything was okay.

'*Di due minuti.*' Luca called, and Meg frowned, throwing her lipstick into her tiny jewelled purse and expecting to race out of the door. 'I've told him we would be two minutes, Meg.'

'But I'm ready….' she called, her voice trailing off as Luca now halted her.

'What I was trying to say, before I was, er, diverted.' Pulling out a slim black box, Luca opened the tiny antique clasp and Meg caught her breath at the beauty of the two jewels that glittered on the plush velvet. Impossibly beautiful, two huge diamonds sparkled in the light, each twinkling at the end of the finest white-gold chain—and she'd have recognised them anywhere.

'They're the jewels I'm supposed to have stolen!'

'The very same.' Luca smiled. 'These were my grandmother's.' Gently Luca lifted them from where they rested, but, reeling, Meg stepped back.

'I can't wear them.' She shook her head. 'Luca, these are your family jewels. I can't possibly wear them tonight— what if I lost one? What if—?'

'They are your jewels,' Luca interrupted. 'This is my gift tonight to you.'

'Luca, no, I can't possibly—'

'You like them?' he interrupted.

'Of course—they're beautiful.'

'And I want you to have them, so there is no problem.'

Spun into confusion, Meg shook her head. 'It's too much, too soon, Luca.'

'Not for me.' He stared back at her. 'And this is not about making you stay, or showing you all you could have—I know you are not that superficial, Meg. I want you to have them because, whatever happens between us, it has been more special than I can say. This gift is yours with no expectations, nothing more than—' He gave a frustrated shrug. 'I would not give these to just anyone—you might not know that, but my family will. I want you to walk beside me tonight and for them to know how precious you are to me. Please, accept them.'

So she did, overwhelmed not just at his generosity and the sentiment behind them, but the apparent fact that Luca felt as strongly as she did—that the feelings that had swept her away since she'd first laid eyes on him had carried him with her, had been as strongly felt by Luca too.

'They're beautiful,' Meg breathed, watching the light capture them in the huge antique mirror above the fireplace, but, as captivating as they were, when Luca came behind her, his hands locking around her waist, burying his face in her neck and kissing his way down over her shoulder, Meg closed her eyes on the image in the mirror, focussing her mind solely on him.

'So are you, Meg.'

She felt it—for the first time in forever she felt beautiful, not just on the outside but somewhere deep within, as if he'd reached inside and polished the rough stone of her heart into a diamond that sparkled more magnificently than the ones he'd just given. This time when he offered his arm, when he checked that she was ready, for Meg there was no hesitation, just anticipation, nowhere in the world she'd rather be than beside this stunning, intriguing man.

Niroli had pulled out all the stops for this most special day— and by evening it was the royal family's turn to thank them, to acknowledge the people of Niroli before the celebrations continued long into the night.

Across Niroli, preparations had been made to feast and party late into the night, to celebrate the riches the fertile soil brought them each year—but first, as was tradition, many of the islanders had come to wait outside Niroli Palace where their royal family would appear, acknowledging the people of Niroli before greeting their guests for the ball.

It was a glittering line-up. The women were lavishly dressed, exquisitely made-up and dripping in gemstones, their opulent perfumes mingling as they gathered on the steps of the palace, whilst the royal men stood suave and resplendent in their tuxedos as the crowd cheered.

This Feast, though, Luca had explained as they'd made their way through the palace, was tinged with sadness. Despite the exuberant crowds, despite the buzz of excitement, for the people of Niroli the fact their king was too weakened to attend made the celebrations bittersweet.

What he didn't add was that tonight, more so than usual, the eyes of Niroli were upon him.

Could Prince Luca Fierezza rule them?

Could the black-eyed wild child they had all simulta-

neously adored and berated through his reckless youth really
be their king?

Their answer was a resounding yes—the cheers deafen-
ing as Luca and the stunning, mysterious woman beside
him joined the family on the steps.

'Trust Luca!' The crowd nudged and cheered. *Trust their
Luca* to add an extra dash of glamour to the night. 'Who is
she?' It was the question on everyone's lips—who was the
gorgeous stranger at Luca's side? Who was this woman who
chatted amicably with Princess Laura? It was a question
that would have the whole town talking and guessing long
into the night!

For Meg, awkward in crowds, nervous of eating in front
of strangers, the night was illuminating. Despite the grand
company she was keeping, despite the endless conveyor belt
of food that would normally have had her breaking out in a
cold sweat, with Luca beside her, it wasn't just bearable—
it was enjoyable! It was as if he'd reached inside her and
turned on a switch, everything brighter, sweeter, more
vibrant—everything just so much easier with him beside her.

'You are enjoying yourself—yes?' They were dancing
now—Meg, who didn't know whether or not she could,
because she'd never attempted a formal dance, was still none
the wiser as to her skill because Luca's lead was so skilled, so
effortless, he more than made up for her lack of experience.

'I am.' Meg beamed up at him, drunk on a single glass of
wine and the intoxicating presence of him. 'It's all wonderful,
the people, the music, the food…' Her eyes caught his. 'You.'

'Tonight, I enjoy myself too.'

'You don't normally?'

He didn't get to answer, the dance finished and the floor
broke into applause. 'Come.' Luca took her hand and

guided her off the floor. 'It is time to introduce you to some more people.'

'More kissing strangers?' Meg gave a tiny little sigh. It would surely take her forever to get used to the effusive Italian greeting of kissing on both cheeks. 'I guess it's so easy for you but—'

'Believe me—' Luca grinned '—on many occasions it is less than easy. My family are not all beautiful.'

This one was, though!

There was a familiar feel to the woman who stepped forward at Luca's bidding. Slightly taller than Meg, she was dressed in a sheath-like golden dress, her thick, honey-blond hair fell heavy and immaculate and without introduction Meg knew she was royal. There was a timeless elegance about her, not just from what she was wearing, but from the way she carried herself, and when Luca introduced her Meg knew where she'd seen her.

'Meg, this is my cousin, Princess Isabella Fierezza.'

The name was as familiar as the face and instantly Meg placed her—Princess Isabella Fierezza frequently graced the pages of glossy magazines, a darling of the paparazzi. The fascination with this stunningly beautiful woman carried around the world, whether sipping coffee in a bar or lying on a sun-drenched beach, her image was newsworthy.

'Please, call me Isabella.' As charming as she was elegant, Isabella dispensed with titles, pulling Meg into the inner sanctum of the royals with surprising ease, and after a moment or two of awestruck awkwardness Meg started to relax, so much so that she didn't mind a scrap when Luca had to excuse himself to attend to a duty dance.

'How are you finding it all?' Isabella asked in excellent English. 'We're a difficult lot to get used to, I'm sure.'

"Everyone's been charming,' Meg answered truthfully. 'Though, I have to admit, I was nervous at first.'

'It will take a while to get used to it.' Isabella nodded her understanding. 'Especially at the moment—the interest in our family is always intense, but never more so than now. There are many eyes watching us….' Was it sympathy in her own eyes as she smiled over at Meg? 'Luca does not like the press—he still seems to wonder why his life is newsworthy. It will be more so now!'

'Because of the king's health.' Meg checked, but surprisingly Isabella shook her head.

'Because there is nothing the press like more than the possibility of a new princess.'

'We've only just met,' Meg responded with a smile, not sure if Isabella was teasing her as Laura had, or was somehow testing her—but she was wrong on both counts.

'You are wearing the Royal House of Niroli jewels, Meg.' Isabella nodded graciously to a rather red-faced couple who were coming off the dance floor, then turned direct hazel eyes back to Meg's. 'Understand that I will not be the only one to notice.' For a second Meg thought she was being warned, that there was something underhand to Isabella's comments, but again she was mistaken. 'If you need to talk—if you would like another woman to talk to when it all gets too much, and,' she added, 'it *will* get too much, then I would be more than happy to help you. Unlike Luca I am used to the press—I know how to work them. Sometimes it is better not to dodge them—'

'Don't believe a word she tells you!' Luca was back, for Meg's sake talking in English as he good-naturedly teased his cousin. 'I was never *that* bad.'

'Oh, yes, you were, Luca—' Isabella smiled, carrying on

the joke '—but I'm too much of a lady to talk about your past. Anyway, why would I scare her off when she's absolutely charming?'

'From my cousin—that was high praise, indeed,' Luca said *much* later when they were back in his apartment, Meg utterly aching and exhausted but reeling from the wonderful night they had shared.

'I liked her.' Meg nodded, sitting up in bed wearing nothing but a smile and talking nineteen to the dozen as an exhausted Luca attempted to close his eyes. 'She's stunning.'

'She works at it,' Luca mused. 'You could learn from her. Not like that!' He laughed as she nudged him angrily in the ribs. 'I'm not talking about how she looks—Isabella manages the press well, manages to be royal and work too.'

'She works?'

'In tourism.' Luca nodded. 'She does well for Niroli…' He didn't get to finish, falling asleep mid-sentence, his expressive face relaxing, dark lashes fanning his cheeks. Given it was 3:00 a.m., Meg probably should have done the same— should have flicked off the night light and cuddled up beside him, only she didn't want this day to end….

Didn't want to close her eyes on the magic she had found.

Nothing.

Waking up, wrapped in his loving embrace, her whole body exquisitely tender from the passion of the day before, Meg took a moment to work out what was worrying her….

Nothing.

Not a single thing on her mind was big enough to detract from what she was feeling now, and as he opened his eyes and smiled back at her Meg knew he was feeling it too.

Safe.

Two ships coming in from the storm at the same time, holding each other as they reached solid ground—revelling in the peaceful harbour they had found.

'Good morning,' Luca greeted her in English.

'*Buongiorno,*' Meg answered, stretching luxuriously, doing absolutely nothing to retrieve it as the sheet slipped from her warm, relaxed body, just sharing a slow, lazy kiss before the busy day invaded.

'Can't we stay in bed for a while?' Meg grumbled as Luca reluctantly climbed out.

'Impossible!' He gave a dramatic Latin gesture but, given he was naked, it merely made Meg giggle. 'We will be expected in the dining room for breakfast.'

'With your family?'

'Don't worry.' Luca waved away her anxiety. 'It will be very informal. There is no need to dress up or worry about make-up and such things.'

'Please!' Meg rolled her eyes. 'Don't send me in there unarmed. I somehow can't picture your cousin Isabella wrapped in a shabby dressing gown, wearing last night's make-up.'

'Probably not,' Luca conceded, 'but it will be very relaxed. No doubt there will be a prolonged discussion about who behaved worst last night....' Seeing Meg's slightly frantic expression, it was Luca's turn to laugh. 'You, Miss Donovan, were impeccable, unlike Countess Arabella....'

'Which one was she?' Meg frowned. 'The one in the salmon-coloured dress who—?'

'Well, she was leaping like a salmon!' Luca grinned. 'But, no, Countess Arabella was the one...' His voice trailed off as there was a knock at the door and he went to answer it. Meg settled back on the bed, still smiling at the many memories from last night. Frankly, for such a dignified bunch, some of their behaviour had been shocking to say the least.

'Your cousin Isabella was nice. She said…' But Meg's voice trailed off as Luca re-entered the room and she saw his unusually pale face, the carefree features of moments ago replaced—his face taut with tension, lines she had never seen before grooved around his eyes as he sat on the bed beside her. 'What's happened?' Meg gasped. 'Luca, what's happened?'

'It is my grandfather, the king…' Meg's mind jumped to the obvious conclusion but, without her even asking, Luca refuted it. 'No, it is not that. He has summoned me.'

'Summoned you?' Meg frowned, not just the language but the whole concept unfamiliar, that a grandfather *summoning* his grandson could cause such a shocked reaction. 'What for?'

'I am about to find out.' He let out a heavy breath as if willing himself calm—and Meg realised then just how huge this was for him.

'This isn't a regular event, I take it?'

'*No.*' He gave a brief shake of his head. 'The fact he has summoned me means that it is royal business that he wants to discuss. I knew this day was coming, I just never expected it now.'

Luca dressed quickly—but the informal attire he had deigned suitable a matter of moments ago was replaced with a suit, his tousled hair smoothed back, a quick grimace in the mirror as he decided if he had time to shave, but another rapid knock at the door put paid to that decision.

'Wait here.' He gave her a thin smile as he kissed her distractedly. 'We'll go down to breakfast together once I have spoken with the king.'

'Are you okay, Luca?' She captured his hand as he went to go and for a second he held it, held it so tightly it actually hurt.

'I don't know,' Luca admitted. 'I don't know what I am hoping to hear when I speak with him. Wait here for me, Meg.' He said it again, only this time with entirely different meaning, pulling her into his arms for the briefest of embraces that protocol would allow, before he went to learn his fate.

'Always,' Meg answered, but it fell on deaf ears, Luca closing the door behind him and heading off to meet with the king, heading off to find out his fate, and as she lay back on the pillows, staring at the ornate ceiling, only then did it dawn on her.

It wasn't just Luca's future that was being decided, but her own.

CHAPTER FOURTEEN

EVERYTHING WOULD CHANGE if Luca was chosen as heir.

Meg knew that.

Somehow she understood that the pressure that would placed on him, on *them*, would increase dramatically if Luca was to be King; understood that they wouldn't be afforded the luxury of a normal dating process—but, Meg pondered, nothing about their relationship to date *had* been normal, and not just because of Luca's status.

Because of the man himself.

The second he'd walked into the kitchen at the casino he'd been constantly on her mind: filling her senses, confusing her, angering her, thrilling her. Like a drug addiction, like the disease that had once consumed her, Luca was *all* she could think about—only there was no danger in this obsession.

Despite the blizzard of emotion Luca so easily triggered, still he put peace into her soul. A peace she'd never really known.

He made her strong.

Strong enough to deal with whatever the future threw at them; strong enough to handle whatever fate had in store.

Almost.

One look at his stricken face as he walked back into the apartment and Meg knew that he was devastated, knew that whatever he'd been told hadn't been pleasant—only time hadn't allowed her the luxury of knowing his true choice in the matter.

'It will be okay.' Crossing the room, she put her arms out to him—whatever the king's verdict, it truly didn't matter, it was the effect on Luca that was her primary concern, and she wanted to impart that, wanted to hold him as he told her his fate.

'Don't!'

The force, the venom in the single word he spat out was so unexpected, so completely out of step with the man who had left just a short while ago, that Meg stepped back as if he'd hit her.

'You have to leave.' He didn't look at her as he said it, *refused* to look at her as he gave her the order, delivered with gusto the one scenario, since the king's summons, that she'd never envisaged.

'I have to leave?' She could barely get the word out, couldn't fathom the change in him. 'Luca, what on earth did he say to you?'

'The truth.' Only now did he look at her, eyes that had recently adored her now unfamiliar as they eyed her with contempt. 'That you are not fit to be Queen. That if I continue to date you then I relinquish any right to the throne.'

'I don't understand...' She was so bemused at the complete change in him, it didn't even enter Meg's head to be angry and, plunged into confusion, she struggled to make sense—to make *him* see sense. 'I didn't steal the jewellery, though, Luca. We sorted that out.'

'Did we?' Luca checked. 'Or is this some magnificent ruse you and your friend have concocted?'

She couldn't believe what she was hearing, couldn't

believe the change in him. Last night he had held her, loved her, promised to be there for her—yet at the king's bidding *everything* seemed to have changed.

'Luca, you know I had nothing to do with the theft. You *know* that,' she reiterated. 'We went over this yesterday—'

'Yesterday is over,' Luca interrupted, shrugging his broad shoulders, splaying his hands open and cruelly dismissing what they had so recently shared. 'Yesterday we were caught up in attraction, lust. Today things change, responsibility catches up.'

'What about your responsibility to me?' White-lipped, she confronted him.

'We have known each other a few days.' Again he shrugged—again he twisted the knife. 'As the king pointed out—I have been a prince all my life.'

'And a bastard, too.' Anger was broiling now. Anger at the way he was treating her, yes, but Meg's anger was turned inward on herself—that she had trusted him, that she had *chosen* to believe him, the bitterest of all pills.

'You will leave now. The royal plane is in use with dignitaries, but there is a charter flight in an hour. It will take you to—'

'I'm not flying anywhere.' She raked a hand through her hair. 'I'll get the boat.'

'You'll do as I say.'

'Never again!' Meg flared, but still she had to know more, to make some sense of this madness. 'What did he say to you, Luca? Please tell me what he said.'

'You really want to know?' Finally he faced her. 'I could be King of Niroli or have you—but never both.'

'So you chose Niroli?'

'Of course.' He gave a scornful laugh—mocked her,

humiliated her, and for Meg it was more than enough, already she was turning away, only Luca hadn't finished with her yet.

'What do you expect here, Meg?' He was shouting now, but it barely sunk in, her mind cruelly slow to process each vile word, like a huge sticking plaster being slowly ripped off the raw surface of her heart. Why couldn't he just end it—just rip it off in one burst instead of prolonging the agony, exposing her raw wounds, so slowly, so roughly they bled all over again? 'You were acting like a *puttana* in the bar the night I met you, a common backpacker, first scrubbing pots in the kitchen, gambling and flirting with rich businessmen—'

'Enough!' Trembling but somehow firm, she raised her hand, halted his hideous tirade with one of her own. 'Whatever you think of me, Luca, I don't want to hear it, because your opinion doesn't matter to me any more.' She thought she was going to vomit, right here on his bloody royal carpet—cold nausea engulfing her—but she refused to suffer any further indignity. She headed to the bedside, the rumpled sheets they had made love within mocking her now, and took a sip of water from a glass by the side of the bed that had been hers for a fraction of time. The nausea receded but a new visitor arrived, one that she'd suppressed for so long, one that she'd never dared act on—till now.

Swinging around, Meg splashed the remains of the glass in his face with as much venom as if she'd spat at him.

'Guttersnipe!' Luca hissed. 'I will tell the king his assessment was correct.'

'Why?' She'd never asked before—never had the courage to confront, but that much he'd given her at least, anger a powerful precursor to courage. Only it wasn't just Luca she was asking the question, her eyes ravaged with all the pain the world had inflicted in her twenty-five years. 'Why, when you could have just slept with me, did you have to make me love you? Why did you have to do it to me all over again?'

'Again?' His eyes narrowed at her question. 'What do you mean again? You cannot compare me to your parents.'

'Can't I?' Meg rasped. 'Why is it that the people who are supposed to care about me, the people who are supposed to love me, are the very people who hurt me? Why did you have to do this?' She thumped her fist to her chest—more Italian in her actions than him. Raw, untapped emotions were unleashed now, her voice rising with each and every passing word. 'I trusted you, Luca—you made me trust you! You're worse than my parents!'

'Worse? How can you say that? Did I starve you? Did I ignore you?' He was attempting to match her fury, but he couldn't. Attempting to justify, but, for Meg at least, he never could.

'Far worse,' Meg said finally, the screaming over, cool detachment in her voice as her contemptuous eyes gave him one final glance. 'At least my parents never pretended to care.'

'Your backpack is in the car....' Luca's complexion was grey, his voice abrupt when he spoke, but he wasn't shouting any more, wasn't even looking at her now. 'Luigi will take you to the airport.'

'I'm leaving on a boat.' Meg stood perhaps not firm, but resolute, the defences she had let him take down snapping into delayed action, her back straightening, tears drying up, and somehow she managed to face him.

'I want my winnings.' She held out her hand—if he thought her nothing more than a tart, then she'd act like one! 'Heaven knows, I've earned them!'

* * *

Luigi took her to the Port of Niroli where she'd arrived such a short while ago—yet it felt as if it had been a lifetime away. As if she were a criminal being deported, Luigi escorted her onto the boat. How she wanted to book a cabin—to curl up in a ball and hide—but she refused to go there again. Refused to even set a foot in the black hole she'd worked so hard to dig herself from.

It had been a lifetime—Meg realised. She'd arrived in Niroli a frightened girl, but was leaving now a woman.

A proud woman.

'Cheese focaccia and a café latte, *grazie*.'

It was the last thing she wanted, yet Meg knew as she ordered it was the most important meal she'd ever eat—the first big step towards moving forward.

Taking her order, Meg made her way onto the deck, sat at one of the white Formica tables and forced herself to carry on with living, and if her nose occasionally ran, or tears were streaming out from under her glasses, if the man opposite was giving her curious looks from over his newspaper as she sniffled her way through her meal, it really didn't matter.

Somehow she'd get through this. When the acute agony of the moment had given way, somehow she'd assimilate it, somehow she'd manage to relegate the last few days to a brief holiday romance. One day, Meg decided, she'd even look back with fondness, gaze at a map and remember dancing and romancing with the Prince of Niroli, perhaps watch the foreign news with a pensive smile....

Just not yet.

The tears were starting again, the gargantuan proportions of the task ahead starting to overwhelm her, because, no matter how much time might dilute the pain, no matter how much it healed, right now she was stuck in the present—his vicious words still stinging in her ears, the brutal force of his rejection still ricocheting in every nerve.

God, she knew she looked a sight, but wouldn't that man stop looking? He wasn't even being discreet, just blatantly staring.

Taking a bite of her food, Meg wished she'd ordered water to wash it down, every morsel sticking in her throat as she struggled to begin her future and, reaching in her bag for her purse, Meg decided to do just that and then take the opportunity to move to another table.

But first she'd have a quick look.

Rarely did Meg need to be reminded these days of her painful past—eating, self-nurturing, coming so much easier, but this morning a few life lessons were needed, and she'd utilise every means available to get her through.

Unzipping the wallet part of her purse, Meg's fingers slipped inside, and she frowned as the well-thumbed photo didn't come to immediate reach, more desperate now as she started to unzip each segment. It was gone; she must have dropped it. Frantically she tried to remember when she'd last seen it…the night she'd met Luca. Panicking now, Meg tipped out her purse's contents onto the table—but everything else was in order….

'*Scusi?*'

Meg tried to ignore the man opposite. Still frantically looking for her photo, she was in no mood to be chatted up, but as he gestured to the newspaper in his hands she realised why he had been staring. There on the front cover, almost unrecognisable in her happiness, she stood resplendent by Luca's side.

'This is you? Yes?'

'No.' Meg shook her head and told the twisted truth. 'She just looks similar.'

Thankfully she'd lost her audience, his attention diverted by a seaplane dipping precariously low on the smooth sparkling ocean, the whole top deck watching as it drew in for landing, but Meg couldn't have cared less, more relieved when her table mate excused himself and, camera in hand, headed to the rails to get a few shots for his album. But curiosity overrode her, and, reaching over, Meg turned the paper around, staring at the image and trying to believe it had only been yesterday. That the radiant, smiling face was hers, that Luca, proud, dignified and gazing down at her with nothing but pride and tenderness in his features, could possibly be the cruel beast she had witnessed this morning.

Scandalo al Palazzo.

Meg's eyes jerked from her and Luca's picture as the headline caught her eye. What scandal?

Some of the guests might have kicked up their heels, but that had been long after midnight, long after any article would have been written and the paper put to bed.

Curious now, wondering what she might have missed, Meg turned the paper around and opened the first page—her inquisitiveness replaced with frozen horror as she stared at the images in front of her. It didn't matter that the article was written in Italian, because Meg knew without translation what had been said—a true case of a picture painting a thousand words. Because there, staring back at her, frail and emaciated, was the fragile, bewildered woman she once had been. The photo she had carried to remind her of her most private pain was a salacious piece of gossip now. The awful realisation sank in that she hadn't lost her photo…it had been stolen.

It was as if the universe were coming out in sympathy—as her heart lurched and Meg's world literally stopped, so too did the boat, the vehicle shuddering as the engines cut, everything falling silent as Meg tried to take it all in.

'Signorina Donovan?' The hesitant tone to the captain's voice, the fact he was addressing her by name, momentarily dragged Meg's eyes away from the article. 'I am sorry to disturb you—this really is most irregular—' He gestured out beyond the deck to the seaplane, bobbing gently on the calm water, as Meg attempted to focus on whatever it was the captain was telling her.

Maybe there had been an accident, perhaps she needed to move.... Gathering up the newspaper, her bag, she tried to stand on legs that seemed to be made of cotton wool, tried polite conversation with a mouth that didn't know how to move, a mind that simply didn't know how to respond.

'He wonders if you would join him. We have a small boat that can take you and naturally we would wait—'

'I'm sorry.' Meg gave a helpless shake of her head. 'Join whom?'

'Crown Prince Fierezza!' When Meg clearly didn't react in the way the captain expected, when, instead of jumping to attention, Meg sat back down, the captain's voice became more insistent. 'This way, *signorina*—he has asked to meet with you.'

'No.' She didn't care that the whole boat was taking pictures, didn't care that the captain was practically dancing on the spot with anxiety—didn't even particularly care that Luca had made this dramatic gesture and landed a seaplane beside the boat, because she had nothing to say to him.

Nothing at all.

'*Signorina*, you cannot just refuse, when our prince requests—'

'*Your* prince,' Meg interrupted. 'Luca Fierezza is *your* prince, not mine. I have absolutely no desire to speak with him.' She cleared her throat, wished, wished, wished she'd made it to the bar to get her bottle of water before all this had happened, and that she *had* booked the tiny cabin and was away from all the curious stares. 'I'm not leaving this boat,' Meg said firmly. 'So if you could kindly pass on that message, then we can start moving again.'

The captain looked as if he were about to have a seizure, Meg's response, or lack of it, clearly diverging from protocol, but he got the message when proudly she headed towards the bar, absolutely refusing to look over her shoulder, to look back on *all* she was leaving behind... focused instead on all she was heading to.

At twenty-five years and four months, Meg grew up.

Not that she'd been immature, not that she'd shirked responsibility for herself—with the cards she'd been dealt Meg had never been afforded that luxury—but in facing her past, somehow she embraced her future.

No, she wasn't perfect and, yes, she'd make mistakes—but from now on each and every one would be her own; the cards she'd been dealt had long since played out.

'*Uno champagne, grazie!*' Meg said to the bar man.

Who cared if it wasn't even midday?

Who cared if the Prince of Niroli was waiting for her to come over?

Who cared what anyone thought? Sitting down at her lonely table, placing a napkin over her knees and taking a sip of her champagne, Meg took a deep breath and smiled at the world.

Her best *was* good enough for her.

'May I join you?'

Well, if he was going to land a seaplane, then it wasn't *that* unexpected that he'd board the boat, and Meg kept her smile in place, gestured for him to sit, a glint of triumph in *her* eyes at Luca's bemused expression.

Because he was a prince, because *nothing* like this had happened on the boat, new strategies were being put in place. The gawking passengers were all relegated to the hull of the boat to give the couple some semblance of privacy, but their cameras aimed, their eager faces all watching on as Meg's plastic cup was removed and replaced with two glass flutes and the boat's best champagne was poured into them. A hastily prepared antipasto platter was placed in front of them and when there was nothing more the boat could pull out to impress, nothing more that could be done, with a flick of Luca's impatient wrist the hovering staff melted away until finally it was just the two of them.

'You are okay?' Luca asked, his voice tentative, glancing down at the open newspaper, then tearing his eyes away.

'Do I look okay?' Meg asked.

'Actually, yes.' Luca gave a slightly bemused frown. 'You have seen…' His voice trailed off and Meg completed the difficult sentence for him.

'The newspaper—yes, I've seen it. I haven't read it as such, but I can imagine what it says. "Shocking past of future Queen—from famine to feast".'

'Surely you're not okay then…' Luca attempted. 'After this morning—'

'Oh, sorry.' Meg fixed him with a steely glare. 'Were you expecting to find me in the foetal position in a cabin, or perhaps with my fingers down my throat—?'

'Meg, please!' One very well-manicured hand tried to halt her, but Meg wouldn't be silenced.

'Well, sorry to disappoint you, Luca. You know, for the past couple of years I've spent my time dreading I'd relapse, dreading how I'd react in a crisis—well, you've actually done me a favour. Since you walked in that kitchen, my life's been nothing but hell and I haven't gone back—if I can survive Niroli I can survive anything. I might even get a T-shirt printed saying just that!'

'Please—do not be facetious. Do not try and make light of this. This photo, this *article*, this disgusting piece of journalism is the reason I sent you away this morning. This is why it was so imperative that you leave—this is the very thing I was trying to protect you from, hoping you would not see.'

'Really?' There was a slightly shrill note to her voice, a disbelieving edge that had Luca frowning. 'Or were you hoping your subjects wouldn't see it?'

'No.' Immediately he shook his head. 'The king summoned me this morning because his press secretary had seen the first version of the papers.' He gave an angry gesture at the filthy paper. '*This* is what I was trying to prevent you from seeing.'

'But you can't!' His frown deepened at her strange answer. 'How can you save me from it? How can you prevent it, Luca, when it's already happened? Like it or not, this *was* me! And if some prison guard wants to make a small fortune raking up my past—'

'It was Jasmine.' He let the words sink in for a moment before softly continuing. 'This is what your friend did to you, Meg.'

And it was so much worse than a drunken mistake, so, so

much worse than a thief trying to cover her tracks, that Meg's bravado left her then, her body racking in quiet spasms as tears begged to be let out, as the world hurled yet another blow.

'This is the price you will have to pay if you are with me, Meg.'

'Would have paid,' Meg wretchedly corrected. 'This is the price I would have paid for you, Luca…but not now. I guess you'd better go and find yourself a more suitable queen….'

'There will be no queen….' Luca grabbed at her hands, but she pulled them away, didn't want him to touch her ever again. 'Because I am not going to be King. He didn't summon me with an ultimatum. That is what I told you so you would leave, so you would never know…'

'Why would you lie?' Meg begged. 'How, after everything we went through, could you think that would be…?' Her voice petered out, watching as his dark, expressive eyes stared at her image in the paper, and finally she saw it.

Saw the shock and pain in his features.

The same shock and pain she felt each and every time she saw the photo herself—but there was something else in his eyes too that took a moment or two to register.

Fear.

The fear of seeing someone you love so very, very ill, and all the guilt, however misplaced, that came with it.

'It was a long time ago, Luca.'

'You told me you will never be recovered.' This time when he reached out for her hands she let him hold them. 'I knew you had been sick, I knew you struggled, but seeing that photo—' It was Luca's eyes filling with tears, Luca struggling to contain his emotions, and Meg understood then what had happened—the terror that had struck him this morning. 'You said you never wanted to go back there—when I saw this photo, I just lost it. All I could think of was getting you away from Niroli—I didn't want to be the one to send you back there!'

'You never could,' Meg said softly. 'That part's up to me.'

'Whether I am a prince or a king the press will always want a story. This is just the start—next it will be that you are adopted, the sister of Alessandro…all your past slowly revealed with only worse to come in the future. Every time you put on weight, or lose an ounce, all your family secrets—'

'Every family has got them,' Meg broke in. '*No* family is perfect.' And, seeing his pain, she spoke a touch more softly. 'Not even royal ones.'

'*Especially* not royal ones!' Luca gave a thin smile, but Meg shook her head.

'Every family has their secrets, their rows, their shame. Well, everyone with an iota of zeal in them. That's why people like gossip—it helps when you find out that the future King of Niroli was dating an anorexic—' he winced at her use of past tense but didn't interrupt '—that Princess Laura—'

'Was beaten by her husband.' This time he did interrupt her, joined Meg in saying the truth out loud, and by boldly shining a light on the dark, murky past, somehow brightened it, chased away the shadows that distorted the images and shrank them to more manageable proportions.

'What *did* the king say this morning, Luca?'

'He said that there was already too much scandal attached to my name—that he'd warned me that one more slip-up, one more piece of scandal, and I would not be considered as the successor.'

'I'm sorry,' Meg said, staring down at her hands, the

vastness of what he was telling her hitting home, and even if it wasn't her fault, somehow she had been a part of his demise, but Luca refused to accept her apology.

'I'm glad.' Luca smiled over at her, but she didn't believe him for a second, knew he was just putting on a front, trying to say the right thing….

Until she looked up.

It was as if a genie had sprinkled some magic dust on him, or some Hollywood surgeon had somehow performed the speediest of makeovers whilst she hadn't been looking, because, staring back at her, looking younger, happier, *sexier* than she had ever seen him, was Luca Fierezza.

Well, maybe not sexier, Meg thought to herself, her mind working on minor details before she cleared her mental in tray to deal with the big tasks that were surely coming to hand—Luca Fierezza had always oozed sex appeal. That had been the problem from the start!

'You're not even a tiniest bit disappointed?'

'No.' Luca shook his head, but his eyes crinkled at the side as he thought a bit deeper. 'Maybe a little,' he admitted. ' I have this huge ego, you see—I have to be the best. I guess when the new king is crowned, or if I feel sorry for myself on New Year's Eve one year…'

'Woe is me.' Meg smiled at his confusion and quickly translated. 'You'll be thinking "poor me".'

'I like the first one,' Luca said stoutly. 'Yes, for five minutes every now and then it will be "woe is me", but, that is a small price to pay for freedom.

'I don't want to be King,' Luca said firmly, his hand gripping hers tightly. 'I told the king that—I said that even without this latest scandal that would have been my decision….' He stared down at the paper, his mouth tightening in a thin, angry line before speaking again. 'I hate them for what they did to you. I don't know how I can stop it.'

'Luca,' Meg said gently, 'do I look like I'm mortified? Do I look as if the world has just ended?'

He stared at her for the longest time, taking in the champagne, the half-eaten sandwich, then, slowly removing her sunglasses, he revealed her reddened eyes.

'Don't pretend it didn't hurt.'

'I'm not,' Meg said softly. 'It hurt like hell, but I *am* okay. Better than okay, actually—I know that I can bounce back now! Of course this hurt me, Luca—' she gestured to the picture '—but it was the change in *you* that was agony.'

'I was trying to protect you.'

'I didn't want you to protect me, Luca,' Meg said sadly. 'I just wanted you to stand beside me.'

'And I will,' Luca urged, 'if you'll let me.'

'I don't think so.' Meg glanced over to the deck, to the passengers all clicking their cameras, thrilled to be witnesses to this most exciting moment and, no doubt, Meg thought with a healthy dash of cynicism, aching for the boat to start so they could get to land and sell the photos! 'If we're together, what happens next time, Luca? Next time the press have their blood up, or you're summoned by your grandfather?'

'There won't be a next time,' Luca started, wincing at the hollowness of mere words, knowing it would take so much more than that to convince her.

'The things you said to me this morning—'

'Were to make you leave—to make you hate me, if that was what it took. It was the only way, or so I thought. Then, when you'd gone, Isabella came to see if you were okay with the newspaper, to see if she could help.'

'She wanted to help?' Meg blinked at the thought that

Isabella, that the stunning, beautiful Princess Isabella, had been prepared to help her through this, that, instead of being furious or angry, she had actually been prepared to be there for her.

'Isabella didn't know you had gone. She came in full of advice, said that we should go to the beach this afternoon—be photographed together happy and carefree—that this would soon pass, but all she was really concerned with was how *you* were, how you were coping with it all. I knew that in trying to help you I had deeply hurt you. When you said I was worse than your parents...' He paused, hoping, praying that she'd intervene, tell him it had been spoken in haste, only she didn't.

'You hurt me deeply, Luca.'

'I know—and I will regret it forever. I will try to make it up to you forever. I was never ashamed of you, Meg. I was scared for you.'

'Truly?'

'Truly.' Luca nodded. 'In fact nothing would make me prouder than responding to the press by telling them that you are my future wife.'

'Wife?'

'Princess Megan Fierezza!'

'It sounds terrible.' Meg giggled, but it faded midway, the magnitude of the moment catching up, and it was all too confusing, too big, too much to take in, and she started to cry instead. 'I don't know if I can trust you again. You're asking me to lay all my cards on the table—'

'Not yet,' Luca interrupted. 'Don't say anything till I have revealed mine....' Meg frowned in confusion, anger almost as he stared at an imaginary hand of cards, laying his first on the table.

'A king of hearts,' Luca said, but Meg angrily shook her head.

'This isn't a game, Luca.'

'I've never been more serious,' Luca said. 'I show you all that I have in my hands, a potential king that really doesn't want to be one. What about you?'

'A heart,' Meg gulped, 'that doesn't know if it can trust you again.'

'What number?' Luca insisted. 'What number is this heart?'

'Two.' Meg plucked a number from air again—no idea where he was leading, but at least in playing along with Luca she had time to think.

'Well, I have a queen of hearts—' Luca took a deep breath '—only she is not happy. What is your next one?'

'Three of hearts,' Meg said, staring boldly at him now. 'Who's not ashamed of her past—and not particularly proud of it either—but learning to deal with it. You?'

'Knave.'

'Sorry?' Meg let out a little laugh. 'You mean the Jack! The scoundrel, the reprobate—'

'The knight in shining armour?' Luca countered. 'If you'll let me be?'

'Four of hearts,' Meg said, evading the question and smiling at his frown.

'You bluff?'

'Nope.'

'What else?' Luca asked.

'It's your call.'

'What else?' Luca insisted.

'I don't know.' She stared at her imaginary hand, tried to fathom what should come next—the joker, perhaps, smiling in the face of adversity, ignorant of the tremendous problems they faced. 'Ace of hearts…' she attempted, but Luca shook his head.

'No, you don't!' The soft pad of his thumb wiped away the single tear on her cheek that had strayed. 'You cannot have that one, because I hold it here. So don't try to bluff me, Meg, because I can read you. I know you are strong, I know you are proud, and I know that you will be okay without me—but I also know you would be so much better with me, as I would be with you. I know that with this hand I will always win.'

'How?' Meg begged. 'How do you know that?'

'This is a royal flush.' Luca placed his imaginary cards on the table and the strangest thing of all was that she actually looked—looked at all he was holding, all he was offering. 'Which is the best combination of all—no one can beat that.'

'No one?' Meg checked.

'Together these cards beat all others.' Luca took her pale, trembling hands and warmed them in his. 'Together we can beat anything.'

She screwed her eyes closed, blinded with indecision, frantically trying to process her thoughts, but when she opened them Luca was still there, still smiling, still patiently waiting for her answer.

'I need lipstick!'

'Scusi?' Clearly it wasn't what he was expecting her to say, but he accepted it without question, handed her her bag and watched in bemused wonder as she ducked behind the beastly newspaper and painted on a glossy smile. 'Better?' Luca checked when she came out from behind.

'Much.' Meg beamed, but her eyes were glittering with tears. She felt happy, scared and nervous all at the same time as she looked out at the frantic passengers. Tired of patiently waiting, they were starting to get restless, and Meg knew that it was time. Taking a deep breath, she held it in her lungs, reaching out for Luca as they prepared to jump together. 'We should get back to the palace.'

'You're sure?' Luca checked, relief flooding his face as he captured her hand in his.

'Very.' Meg nodded, nerves strangely settling as she stood up and he slipped his free hand around her waist and guided her out to the cheering crowd, cameras flashing, a hundred well-wishers capturing this precious moment.

As *their* Luca brought forth his future bride.

EPILOGUE

'IS EVERYTHING to your satisfaction, Your Royal Highness?'

'*Sì.*' Luca nodded, barely glancing up from the magazine he was reading as the air steward refreshed his glass, but when she asked the same question of Meg, used her very new, very unfamiliar formal title, Meg could only manage a blush, cringing as the steward melted away.

'We're supposed to be going to Australia to escape all this.' Meg gulped. 'I'll never get used to it.'

'I'm sure if you ask she can find you a seat back in economy,' Luca drawled, but, seeing Meg's rigid expression, he stopped teasing her.

As Luca had feared, the press had been merciless and, seeing the needless anguish it was causing, tired of the constant barrage of intrusion, he had made a decision—a huge one: he was leaving Niroli to start a new life in Australia on the Gold Coast where he already had more than a few business ventures.

'They've got a passenger list,' Luca explained. 'My title's on my passport—of course they're going to use our titles, but once we get to Australia we'll just blend in.'

'I doubt it.' Meg stared over at her new husband and,

despite her nerves, found herself smiling—Luca could never 'just blend in' even if he didn't use his title, or reside in a palace. Even without his bodyguards or legions of adoring subjects, Luca would always stand out from the crowd, would always turn heads wherever he went.

'Won't you miss it?'

'Miss what?' Luca shrugged. 'Having my private life sprawled over the magazines? Being told how to behave, how to react?'

'Your family,' Meg pushed, sure he was putting on a brave face, that walking away from Niroli and all he had there, all that he *was* there, surely couldn't be that easy. But as he took her hands in his and gazed so deeply into her eyes it was as if he were inside her, Meg realized, with clarity so bright it blurred the edges, that he wasn't putting on a front—that here, *anywhere*, with her was where Luca wanted to be.

'You are my family,' he said solemnly. 'You come first, last and always, Meg.'

The intensity of his love was overwhelming, but it didn't daunt her now—it soothed her. The strong backdrop he provided was a delicious constant for all that would follow— life's journey an exciting adventure, not a daunting passage, with Luca by her side.

'What do you think *your* family make of it all?'

'I have no idea,' Meg admitted. 'First they had Alex's bombshell to deal with, and now this!'

'I joked to your father on the phone that when I asked for your hand that he wasn't losing a daughter but gaining a princess. Do you know what he said?' Luca didn't wait for her response. 'That he already had one.'

Meg's eyes filled with tears at the thought of seeing her parents and brother again, showing them the proud, beautiful, happy woman she had finally become—and all thanks to love.

Their love and Luca's.

* * * * *

*As the fight for the crown continues on Niroli,
somewhere a man learns that the only life he knows
has been a lie...and that a new life awaits him....*

As she told him he almost didn't need to listen. Almost.

Looking at her, he could see her lips moving, forming the words, but he didn't need to hear them. He needed to see them. To see her eyes, to understand the feelings that wrapped around those words. He needed to see her hands as they shook with fear and release. He needed to watch her breath as she struggled to tell him what he already knew.... The blood running through his veins belonged to a man he'd never met. And from the way she looked, the way her hands twisted the cloth in her lap and the way her words held something more than regret, he knew that one day he would meet that man. The man she loved.

But in this instant, his world crashed like the breaking of the waves. Hard, fast, magnificently. His mother, the only woman he had ever trusted, was the woman who had told him the biggest lie of all. But like the waves the impact was quick, devastating while it lasted, but swiftly drawn back into the calm surface of the sea.

He walked over and laid his hand over hers in a gesture that told her he understood. But he never quite met her gaze.

* * * * *

*Why would a mother lie to her child and who
is the mystery man? More is revealed in book four of*
THE ROYAL HOUSE OF NIROLI,
THE TYCOON'S PRINCESS BRIDE.

Always passionate, always proud.

**The richest royal family in the world—
a family united by blood and passion,
torn apart by deceit and desire.**

By royal decree, Harlequin Presents is delighted to bring
you The Royal House of Niroli. Step into the glamorous,
enticing world of the Nirolian royal family. As the king
ails he must find an heir…each month an exciting new
installment follows the epic search for the true Nirolian
king. Eight heirs, eight romances, eight fantastic stories!

THE TYCOON'S
PRINCESS BRIDE
by Natasha Oakley

Isabella can't be in the same room as Domenic Vincini
without wanting him! But if she gives in to temptation
she forfeits her chance of being queen…and will tie
Niroli to its sworn enemy!
Available October wherever you buy books.

Be sure not to miss any of the passion!
EXPECTING HIS ROYAL BABY
by Susan Stephens
available in November.

REQUEST YOUR FREE BOOKS!

2 FREE NOVELS PLUS 2
FREE GIFTS!

PASSION GUARANTEED SEDUCTION

YES! Please send me 2 FREE Harlequin Presents® novels and my 2 FREE gifts. After receiving them, if I don't wish to receive any more books, I can return the shipping statement marked "cancel." If I don't cancel, I will receive 6 brand-new novels every month and be billed just $3.80 per book in the U.S., or $4.47 per book in Canada, plus 25¢ shipping and handling per book and applicable taxes, if any*. That's a savings of close to 15% off the cover price! I understand that accepting the 2 free books and gifts places me under no obligation to buy anything. I can always return a shipment and cancel at any time. Even if I never buy another book from Harlequin, the two free books and gifts are mine to keep forever.

106 HDN EEXK   306 HDN EEXV

Name	(PLEASE PRINT)	
Address		Apt. #
City	State/Prov.	Zip/Postal Code

Signature (if under 18, a parent or guardian must sign)

Mail to the **Harlequin Reader Service®**:
IN U.S.A.: P.O. Box 1867, Buffalo, NY 14240-1867
IN CANADA: P.O. Box 609, Fort Erie, Ontario L2A 5X3

Not valid to current Harlequin Presents subscribers.

Want to try two free books from another line?
Call 1-800-873-8635 or visit www.morefreebooks.com.

* Terms and prices subject to change without notice. NY residents add applicable sales tax. Canadian residents will be charged applicable provincial taxes and GST. This offer is limited to one order per household. All orders subject to approval. Credit or debit balances in a customer's account(s) may be offset by any other outstanding balance owed by or to the customer. Please allow 4 to 6 weeks for delivery.

Your Privacy: Harlequin is committed to protecting your privacy. Our Privacy Policy is available online at www.eHarlequin.com or upon request from the Reader Service. From time to time we make our lists of customers available to reputable firms who may have a product or service of interest to you. If you would prefer we not share your name and address, please check here. ☐

HP07